Junius Lackland Hempstead

The Conspirator

A Tragedy

Junius Lackland Hempstead

The Conspirator
A Tragedy

ISBN/EAN: 9783337183127

Printed in Europe, USA, Canada, Australia, Japan

Cover: Foto ©Andreas Hilbeck / pixelio.de

More available books at **www.hansebooks.com**

THE

CONSPIRATOR.

A TRAGEDY,

IN FIVE ACTS.

BY JUNIUS L. HEMPSTEAD,

MEMPHIS, - - TENN.

DRAMATIS-PERSONÆ.

Guido.—The Conspirator.
Zelia.—Guido's daughter.
Count of Zeno.—Guido's friend.
Antonio.—The old fisherman.
Duke.—Ruler of Venice.
Doge-Falereo.—2d Ruler.
First Council.
Second   "
Third   "
Fourth   "
Fifth   "
Sixth   "
Seventh   "
Eighth   "
Ludovico.—Alfonso's friend.
Bernado.—A young noble.
Farola.—A Young noble.
Signio.—Hostler of St. Marco's Square.
Alfonso.—A villain and noble.
Silvia.—Zelia's old nurse.
Leoni.—A young noble.
Bertrand.—Antonio's son.
Page.—Alfonso's servant.
Bruno.—Foreman.
First Monk.
Portio.—Guido's spy.
Mario.
Doge's Scribe.
Citizen.
Claud.—Mario's brother, first brother.
Lucretia.
Deppo.—Captain of the guard.
Priest.—Who married A. and M.
Guards, Greeks, Turks, Jews, Pages, &c.

THE CONSPIRATOR.

Guido.—Venice. Oh, proud Venice! what-ever changing fate led me blind-folded to your shores? Why did I leave a land of freedom—my childhood's happy home? The mountains kissed the clouds, and they lingering lovingly, around those hoary-headed anthems of eternal liberty-a union of the gods and men—your aged heads were crowned with heaven's own diadem. My father's cot upon the mountain's side, a sheltering nook, a babbling brook, a life of freedom and of joy—all, all crowd upon my memory now, till thought is madness and madness pain. The dreams of childhood, come back to me with a thousand brilliant charms. I climbed the rugged cliffs, and scaled the mountain's side, plucked the wild flowers from the shaded vale, and played from sun to sun. My brother, too, a comely lad, and sure of foot as I, was ever my companion true, and always by my side; forty years have sped them by—long years they've been to me. We parted on that fatal morn; shuddering I recall the boyish quarrel, the angry words, the struggle and the awful fall.

Zelia.—Father, father! why do you look so strange?—such vacant eyes and horrid stare!—speak to me, speak to your child?

Guido. Nothing, Zelia, nothing; I was but dreaming of the days gone by. How is my child to-day? Does the lagging sunbeams creeping so slowly o'er the palace walls of proud old Venice find thee in health and strength?

Zelia.—I have been up an hour or more, watching the swift gliding gondolas as they skim through these watery streets; how strange a city on the sea—few bestir themselves—all Venice sleeps.

Guido.—Most true; all Venice sleeps; the lion of St. Mark doth guard them well. Bacchus' courts Morpheus, and Morpheus holds them firmly. They dream away, the best part of their days and lives. Their masters in their guarded palaces can well say all Venice sleeps. Be thou my child ever up betimes, to catch the morning breeze, 'twill brighten the roses on thy velvet cheeks; all nature seems more fair. Dost love thy father, child, and wilt thou ever be, the same good child to me, or will thy heart be filled with cankering care, to rob thee of thy roses and thy youth.

Zelia.—How could I ever love thee less? for I have never known a mother's tender, loving care; you have been both to me. The last childish prattle, the slumbering drowsy lid, the upturned good-night glance were all for thee—pillowed on thy strong, broad breast, my sleep was sweet indeed.

Guido.—Thou art wondrous fair to-day, and all Venice would so say. Be brave of heart, my child; take not the shadow for the substance; would that I had a cerberus to guard thee from the living, as he guards the forgotten dead. To your room my child, I'll to my work. (Exit Zelia.) The vicious, untamed, depraved youths of Venice, shall never snatch my treasure from me. Who can tell? we are but human after all, and have been so for four thousand years. The very heart so loyal to me now, may cause me grief in years to come—did I say years? it may be only months.

Zeno.—Good morrow, Guido; what ails thee man? art brooding o'er thy cares? Come, smile, be proud; no arm in Venice is so strong, no rapier so true: a buckler for thy cradle, thy childish toy a blade.

Guido.—Zeno, forgive me: I was dreaming of the past.

Zeno.—'Tis of the past I'd speak, from whence came you—your proud and haughty bearing; Ill bespeaks a near approach to confidence.

Guido.—I want no friends, distrusting friendship much. I command respect, 'tis all I ask or give.

Zeno.—Beware of such a speech, the day will come, when you will feel the want of one, and maybe more.

Guido.—The eaglet was not more free than I; the deer more fleet of foot; no readier blade to do or dare: I lived on freedom's air. All is changed; the very palace walls have ears; suspicion and distrust walk arm in arm; a man dare not say his soul's his own; the revenues of State are all absorbed by theft; argus-eyed vigilance eternal watch is keeping. The rack, the torture, have done their work; we are a republic only in name. Down with the Doge, and his much dreaded council of ten; they are tyrants; death to them.

Zeno.—Silence is liberty in Venice. Had thou saidst as much to other ears, the proud eaglets wings, were closely clipped, the bridge of sighs, would soon convey thee to a dungeon deep.

Guido.—I care not, Zeno, the end must come; argus-eyed vigilance, eternal watch is keeping—not on the ducal treasury; this cruel, iron-handed Doge and handful of robed murderers squander it in a thousand ways. Their spies, an army in themselves, are all well fed and kept, ready for their master's bidding. Base hirelings that they are, miscreants, cowards—only brave in numbers. The gorgious trappings of the palace guard, all glittering in the noon-day sun; their sumptuous larders well filled with stores of wine and luxuries; their tables groan beneath the weight of dainties that would shame an eastern prince. For their amusement all Venice dances and will sing; we are slaves—base slaves; the yoke fits well, then let it stay.

Zeno.—'Tis most true; 'tis most human, and always will be so. Man must govern and men be governed.

Guido.—Why not overthrow this handful of petty tyrants, clothed with some brief authority. They are a stain upon proud Venice; times were not thus, when first my wandering footsteps sought these fair shores. All was liberty then, that is but slavery now; the four hundred and eighty electors of this free people are reduced to ten. Centralization and the torture have done their work. The people with abject fear, have given up one vested right, then another, till all is lost. Eternal liberty, is the price of eternal vigilance.

Zeno.—I pray thee, Guido, for thy sake, beware, you tread on dangerous ground, and invite the council's wrath and torture.

Guido.—The surest throne, is in the people's heart; more liberty of speech, more field for action, the will of the people should be the nation's laws; they should guard well these rights.

Zeno.—Hush, for God's sake hush; the very air will send thy words to listening ears, and then good-by to thy fair thoughts of freedom, and reform.

Guido.—Their shrouded council, seated with closed doors, and guarded with mailed hands, could ne'er withstand the gorgeous light of day. Their deeds are darkness and therefore night.

Zeno.—I love thee well, and were not for thy manly arm, the soul of Zeno had taken flight, his body food for worms. Speak no more of things we cannot help, 'tis at the peril of thy life.

Guido.—You overrate the little service I have done—not worth the thought. The time may come, when I will try thy proffered friendship to the last degree.

Zeno.—It will stand the test, and by all the gods I swear my sword, and fortune, are thine to command, until we meet again. Good by. (Exit.)

Guido.—He has gone: a truer heart beats not beneath a doublets silken fold. He would be a man, but for the brawling times, the sparkling wine, the ribald jest, the women bold and free. They cast a spell upon our better selves, a blow, a quarrel, and a rapier thrust—all is over—we are but dust.

Antonio.—I am here, friend Guido, for a little help; old and feeble, with gray hairs and tottering to his fall, the old man asks for bread.

Guido.—Where is thy son, Antonio? hast been unfortunate with his net, or has the sea gone dry?

Antonio.—He has not fished these many days; he is far too grand for that. I see him seldom, then 'tis late. He was so brave and true, till evil companions, gaming, and bad wine, have so completely turned his head, he cursed his poor old father because he asked for bread.

Guido.—I'll seek, Antonio, for your erring son; it needs

but a word, to recall the manliness that not long since held
sway, o'er that misguided heart.

Antonio.—I'll bless you, Guido, bless you, with my latest
breath; your very name is reverenced in all Venice, for the
noble deeds you have done.

Guido.—Pardon, old man, you have not broken fast, enter,
and partake of Guido's cheer; another soon will fill Antonio's
place. The tree is tottering to its fall; those old eyes have
seen the rise and fall of many a Doge's rule, and may see at
least one more.

Scene.—[In the council chamber, all seated in their places
and in appropriate dress, the Duke in the middle, five on
each side, Pages, Guards and Messengers.]

Duke.—Good day, my worthy council. How fares Adriatics fair queen to-day? Our ships well ladened from the
Levant—bring wealth and commerce to our doors. Our
well-sailed ships—they whiten every sea. Venice is great,
and mistress of the world.

Doge.—Passing well. Our faithful spies, report a quiet
night. Nothing has transpired worthy of great mention.
These good people frolic and drink wine. The women gossip
and dress fine. They are but children after all. If we but
keep them well amused, we have naught to fear. We have
no malcontents to stir—the surface of a smooth and glossy sea.

First Council.—There is one—you all know him well—(at
least by reputation)—Guido by name—an armorer of great
renown, of which all Venice should be proud. Orders for
his suits of mail come from all kingdoms, and all climes.
He has the secret, that is a fortune in itself, of so tempering
steel, with half the weight of other cumbrous suits, they
double in resistance.

Duke.—Well, what of that? Would that we had more of
his kind. It would our revenues increase—of which we
greatly stand in need.

First Council.—Why not seize his shop, and run this work
ourselves? It is a secret, that should belong alone to Venice.
It will throw a lustre on our arms abroad, and make us feared
at home. I like him not. None know from whence he
came. He may be a Genoaian in disguise—from the Devil,
and all such. Our patron saint deliver us.

Doge.—Well to the point.

First Council.—He has high notions of Knight-errantry—
would rather crack a helmet with a battle-axe, than woo the
fairest maid. Rather with a lance in rest, and visor down,
meet in the deadly shock and unhorse men, than play the
gallant to some lady fair.

Second Council—I thank the gods, that Venice swims upon
the Adriatic sea. I like not too much land—the neighing
steed—the mailed knight—and battle-cry. Ugh!! they make
my blood run cold.

First Council.—The people, old and young, think him a very god, and worship at his shrine. No gay young noble, but would give a kingly crown for such an arm, and such a blade. He has captured all hearts by his princely bearing: always on the side of weakness, and against the strong.

Third Council.—He is a dangerous man, and should be closely watched.

First Council.—The Count of Zeno swears by him—for to this Guido, Zeno owes his life. He keeps his counsel, and his tongue. His money, without stint, he gives to the poor—while we with little mercy, tax from door to door.

Fourth Council.—He mocks and derides Venetian ways—calls us women, and not men. Civilization brings refinement; and with refinement, all our martial deeds, give place to gallant speeches, dress, fair women, and old wine—so let it be, at least for me.

Doge.—Forewarned is forearmed—I'll so instruct our spies.

First Council.—His bearing, and his well stored mind, ill befit his calling. I like him not: a fire-brand, ready for the burning.

Fifth Council.—I know him, and of his deeds I well can speak. No braver heart among your Highness' subjects; no one can say aught of his good name. He tends his business close—has no liking for the mid-night brawl. A more peaceable, unoffending citizen dwells not in Venice.

Duke.—Why, half the day is done, our work scarce begun. One would think this valiant knight was at our very doors, with sword in hand, to slay us all. No more of this; I have need of your good counsel. As you well know, our money bags are empty—our guards, and spies, have not been paid. Discontent will follow soon enough. All this glittering pomp, and well-guarded power, makes paupers of us all, and strains our credit to the last degree. These standing armies in times of peace take bread from peoples' mouths, and support the very men who should bring us wealth by toil.

Doge.—Your Highness forgets our neighbors of Genoa. Jealous of our fame, they would make short work of Venice; her wealth of marble palaces; her shipping, and her commerce. We are not over-loved in Venice, as you well know, and need these troops to keep our people down. Without them, we are lost.

Duke.—How can we raise some money? Everything is taxed. Can some fertile brain! devise some scheme.

Fourth Council.—Have we ever taxed ourselves? Gods so forbid. We are the rulers of proud old Venice. To tax ourselves would be an insult to the people. It must come some other way.

Sixth Council.—The Jews——the crucifiers—the money bags of St. Marco's square, and the Rialto—they toil not; neither do they spin. When shall the tax begin?

Seventh Council.—Old shylocks, with their hoarded wealth
—we will bleed them well. Their yellow turbans, and red
hats, are thick as Vampire bats: and, like them, suck our
blood, while soothing us to slumber, with the flutter of their
wings.

Eighth Council.—Their business is more prosperous, than
any in all Venice—which speaks not well for us.

Duke.—A forced loan, then, let it be. Poor, friendless
Jews! The church and state thy foes. The strong oppress
the weak—might makes right, and right makes conquest and
so the world moves on.

Doge.—Our ducal guards, our retinue of spies, and menial,
make the cost of government immense. How can it be
otherwise. The velvet glove, on a hand of iron, serves these
base plebeians well, and seats royalty securely on the throne.
Amuse, but keep them down. Make them feel your power.
There is not a whisper that floats upon the midnight air,
that comes not straight to us.

Duke.—We cannot trust these inoffensive people, then, and
need only fear, to make them abject slaves. Would that our
law was less severe—more merciful. We rule them with an
iron hand. The wretch who stands before the council is
condemned, before he is fairly tried. These dreadful instru-
ments of torture, so grimly silent stand, are monuments of
blood and shame. Those gloomy dungeons, where all hope
has fled, and where the Adriatic sea, idly breaks against those
prison walls, tells them that all things but man are free—
man's inhumanity to man. His God created soul for freedom, and the mind for thought. God's precious gifts, bring
down the wrath of Kings upon them; and all these horrors
are for man, and man alone. Prometheus' stolen fire
brought not happiness, but woe.

Doge.—Your Highness must be jesting, or a woman's weakness steals upon your heart. You cannot govern Venice,
with such thoughts as thine.

Duke.—We are a Republic only in name. There seems
to be no feeling of revolt; no conspirators to hatch high
treason in their dens. Then why so many fawning, cring-
ing attendants, who serve us for our gold to-day, and to-
morrow tear us limb from limb. Confidence begets confidence. We distrust them, and they distrust us.

Doge.—Well, so let it be, and be it must. Our iron hand
shall still strike terror to their conspiring souls; our grasp
shall not relax upon their unwilling purses. We curse the
boat, that weathers the storm, and brings us safe to land.

Duke.—As you will. I would rather be enthroned in the
hearts of this good people, than rule them with a tyrant's rod.
I'll hence, and sign the tax decree—affix the ducal seal. See
thou 'tis well and truly kept.

SCENE.—[In Guido's house.—Enter, Alfonso, Ludovico,
Bernado, Farota, Signio.]

Alfonso.—Fair greetings to you, Guido. How goes the day with thee?

Guido.—Most fair indeed. Dame fortune is most cheery of her smiles. My business prospers. I have more orders than I well can fill.

Alfonso.—How is this? The world's at peace. I hear of, no clash of arms.

Guido.—The world soon will not be—a crusade on the turbaned Turk. A conflict is close at hand, all Europe turns with hungry eyes. A treasure so very rare, a prize so great, she covets and will grasp, though seas of blood be shed.

Ludovico.—You speak in riddles, Guido. What mean you? We are dull of ear in grand old Venice. Foreign news moves slow.

Guido.—The Savior's tomb to be reclaimed, forsooth. What care we for the casket, since the precious jewel's flown? The crescent, and the cross, in deadly conflict soon will be. Though I like not the foolish cause, the very thought of mailed knights, mounted on their fiery steeds, their pennons proudly floating o'er their glittering hosts—the sword, the battle-axe, and spear. They thrill my very blood with joy. It tingles to my finger-tips.

Ludovico.—Yours is a foolish dream. For my part, I'd rather dwell at peace with all the world—in these marble walls of proud old Venice—content to sip old Flemish wine, live on sumptuous fare, and woman's smile to cheer the lagging hours, than ride to death in the whirling, wheeling charge—horse and rider down, the corselet punched, the helmet cracked, their mirrored surface smeared with Ludovico's brains.

Alfonso.—They would strike deep indeed to find so rare a thing. What say you, Signio? Ha! ha! ha! (Laughs.)

Signio.—Ha! ha!! ha!!! You are right, Alfonso. A Turkish cimeter is not more keen than Alfonso's jest.

Ludovico—I like not jesting over much, Alfonso. Be they much or little, they will rest at peace, in this good shell of mine.

Farota.—Shell—ha! ha!! ha!!! 'Tis quite the word. It is a shell indeed.

Ludovico.—Peace, fools! your glib tongues anger me. Your senseless jests fall flat upon my ears, and were not worth a rapier thrust.

Guido.—Peace, young gallants. This is my place, humble tho' it be. Forget not you are only guests. 'Twere better to fall in square, and manly fight, than on some quiet spot, stuck through and through—an unharnessed corpse, a senseless thing.

[*Zelia*—Knocks.]

Guido.—Enter, Zelia—(by all the gods that ever cursed this earth, I am undone. Oh, unpropitious fate! Oh, direful

fortune! I'd rather thrown a thousand ducats in the sea.)
[All this aside.]

Guido.—My daughter, gentlemen—an only child, whose
mother died so young, she scarce remembers the day. I have
been both to her.

What ails thee, child? and to what am I indebted for this
untimely call?

Zelia.—I was lonesome, father, and did tire of Silvia's
presence, and my work. It is not often that I see thee now.
Drive me not back—you do not love me as of yore.

Alfonso.—Pardon, good Guido. I am dazed, blinded, by
this vision. How is this? A flower so beautiful and rare,
sees not the light of day. She is the peer of Mari by great odds.

Guido.—She is but a child in years—time enough to make
or unmake her happiness.

Ludovico.—By heavens, she is more fair than dreams. I
am pleased, smitten, slain by Cupid's tender shafts. 'Tis
some picture, to vanish in thin air.

Farota.—How could such beauty be concealed, and in
Venice, too. 'Tis most strange, and yet most true.

Zelia.—You are welcome, noble sirs, to my father's house.
We have good cheer, and wine; and, best of all, content.

Alfonso.—Fair Zelia is the jewel—most dazzling. The
casket is a worthless thing, I ween, and my eternal hate
upon it, that so long hid, so fair a queen.

Zelia.—You are smooth of tongue, good Seignior. My
thanks extend no further than the gallant speech deserves.

Alfonso.—Then take it for its worth—I'll be content.

Zelia.—So let it be.

Ludovico.—Your pardon, fair Zelia; and may I ask, if in
your childish heart, there lurks no keen desire—no wish to
mingle with the worldly throng.

Zelia.—Give me time to think. A maiden's heart's a foolish thing, and changeful as the wind.

Ludovico.—If you so will, it shall be done. The ducal balls
are grand. Rounds of pleasure never cease. Light-hearted
Venice always on the wing.

Guido.—Light-headed as well. I thank you, gentlemen,
for your interest in my child. There is time enough for all
these frivolous things.

Alfonso.—We will, one and all, say good bye, and for myself, will ever pray that we shall meet again. (Exit all.)

Guido.—My child, it grieves me, that you should have met
these senseless, hair-brained fops. They are not men, but
things, created to suit these effeminate times—idlers, babblers,
ever on the alert, to break some woman's heart; or, empty
flagons, and the midnight brawl.

Zelia.—They were your guests, my father; and as such, de-
served recognition at my hands.

Guido.—So is Antonio, the fisherman, and all, from high to low degree. They come on business. This does not admit them to my inner life, or to my daughter's presence.

Zelia.—Are they, then, so black of heart? They are so handsome in my eyes, and have the proud bearing of Venetian nobles.

Guido.—Judge not man by dress, but by his actions, in this transitory life. I fear my daughter is not pleased with home, and friends; and like the birdling, try her unfledged wings only, to fall to earth, a helpless lump of sinful clay.

Zelia.—I am as happy, as I well can be; my music, tapestry and teacher occupy my entire time. My father's love is all I wish for, or can ask, and yet methinks, there steals upon me, now and then, the sadness of a lonely life; companionship I crave—some one of my age. Silvia is old, though kind of heart and true.

Guido.—You are right, my child, we are young but once; who shall it be? I'll find some worthy girl. Antonio's daughter is of your age—a charming, guileless girl—besides they are so very poor. It shall be so, my Zelia.

Zelia.—I thank you, father, thank you. I'll to my childish duties; would that I were fully grown, to wear such handsome dresses, long trails, jewels and Venetian vails.

Guido.—You shall; my child, and now good bye. (Kisses: exit Zelia.) This sweet, sweet flower, I have watched with tender care---the bud, the blossom and now the full blown rose; the blast of winter strikes deep into my soul, and leaves it leafless, agonized and bare; the rose is blighted and soon will fade. The poisoned arrow's flight has been most true; the seeds of discontent are sown; her face so beautiful and fair, her heart so pure and free, can never stand the fierce onslaught of these corrupting times. A woman's heart's a strange, strange thing, a ribbon, a piece of lace, a jewel rare, a constant thirst for that they do not own, surfeited possession, and a wish for more, quick intuition, and desire to please; they probe the wounded spot, with quick precision, and leave the heart forlorn. (Rings for Silvia). I'll call good Silvia up, her wise counsel will help me much.

Silvia.—Noble master, I wait your good commands.

Guido.—Why, noble Silvia! I am a base plebeian born; there is a wide gulf between them, in Venice.

Silvia.—Nobility of heart is all from God. Nobility of title is a brutish thing, and covered by fine clothes. God's noblemen are rare. Venetian nobles are as thick as clowns, upon some festal day.

Guido.—Purity of heart counts little now, good Silvia. These degenerate times nature's noblemen are rare. About my child I wish to speak. I have been so engrossed in business, have quite neglected Zelia. Tell me, seems she happy and content? Zelia is a child no longer, a woman's shadow, overspreads a childish heart; be vigilant. I trust to your good care; she is my cherished idol; God forgive my love for her, if 'tis sinful, forgive again.

Silvia.—She is not content; she asks more questions in one hour, than I well could answer in a week, of Venice, and her motley throng, from every clime, and tongue, and drinks the answers as some drink old flemish wine.

Guido.—I thought as much; give me your advice—what shall I do?

Silvia.—Go with her yourself, and let her see these sights. Give her fine clothes, and jewels rare, for you are well able.

Guido.—The richest man in Venice to-day, and made it all myself.

Silvia.—Let her be surfeited, and then you'll hear no more of this, and if you go not yourself, why, some one will.

Guido.—How can I mix in such a motley throng, of shallow pates, idiots, fools, puppets, who strut upon life's stage, and with singed wings they die? Will my child pass through all this unscathed? My good heart tells me it is wrong. Whoever deceives this sweet and lovely child, shall my full vengeance feel. Woe to the wretch again, I say doubly woe to thee.

Silvia.—You will be so proud of Zelia; her face the fairest in all Venice. She'll turn the hearts of old, and young, and lead captivity captive in her train.

Guido.—I wish not to measure strength, or break a lance. I am content to cry me quits already; I have no time, for such foolish pastime; my business now so prosperous, would soon melt away. What would my humble friends in Venice, think of stern, and unrelenting Guido, transformed into some jesting clown? It can never be. Silvia, I trust her to your care and watchful eyes; let nothing escape you; indulge her as you will. My child's happiness is all I live for or can ask.

Silvia.—As you so say, it shall be done. (Exit.)

Zeno.—Give me your hand, friend Guido, and a friendly shake. Your hand is feverish, some internal fire consumes thee and needs the leeches craft; what ails thee, art sick?

Guido.—Sick unto death. Sick in mind, body and in spirit. The time has come, or is it coming, that will try my very soul.

Zeno.—What has happened, tell me Guido?

Guido.—I told thee not long since, I wished not for friends; I feel the need of one to-day.

Zeno.—I'll be thy friend and be most glad. What can I do for thee? Come, speak.

Guido.—Much friend Zeno, much. I have an only child, whose face so fair, will yet be my curse. Just budding into womanhood, she wishes, sighes and feels most sad, because she's lonely, and would see the sights. How can I trust her, so frail a bark, would soon be wrecked upon so rough a sea?

Zeno.—You take life's troubles all too much to heart; there are other daughters in the world, and other father's too. Borrow not trouble from the future, or it will repay thee with gray hairs.

Guido.—Not like mine; she ne'er has had a mother's watchful care, and woman's quick tuition, to tell the right from wrong, to pick the gold, from heaps of dross.

Zeno.—She will weather the storm I ween. Give her the chance, an untried saintly soul, deserves no credit from on high: with no temptation comes no sin, and with no sin no fall, and with no fall no devil.

Guido.—Did harm come to my darling child, I'd turn all Venice up side down.

Zeno.—I doubt it not, and only ask delay, and safety, till that time does come.

Guido.—I like not these piping times of peace: we are behind the age. All Europe's armed and ready for the fray, while we sit moping, with no soul above the fragrant wine— no hearts for brave and manly deeds; it brings a blush of shame for Venice, who well could spare ten thousand men.

Zeno.—Softly, Guido, you are boiling over, and no fire beneath the caldron either. The world's all wrong with thee to-day. Many a brave spirit dwells in Venice, though now debauched with wine and game, would be foremost in the deadly charge. Some one to rouse this latent manliness, and this sleep of wine once broken, Venice would be proud indeed to own such daring knights.

Guido.—Come sup with me, the day is on the wane, the shadows thicken and grow deep along the palace walls, the gondolier's shrill signal, is all that's heard; there is light and cheer within, I have much to say to-night. (*Enter.*)

Scene.—[In St. Marco's Square, near Signio's.]

Alfonso.—So, so, easy, good fellow, there is a ducatoon for thy trouble; land me safely on Signio's marble stairs. I am late already; the nights are long, thank God, and well drawn out; they are equal to a week. (*Knocks and enters.*)

Signio.—Welcome. Alfonso, thrice welcome to my hall; few have come in to-night, we will have a quiet game, and may dame fortune smile to-night upon thee. (*Knocks, repeated knocks. Enter Ludivico, Farota, Bernado, Lioni, Bertrand.*)

Signio.—Now all the gods be praised for this; we will have a rousing night. Sit round this table, and I'll call for wine. Waiters, ho! waiters! Bring wine—give us my best, 'tis ambrosia for the gods. Let Bacchus reign supreme, we will be the votaries at his shrine, and Mercury help us in our game.

Alfonso.—This is good wine, and fit for any Grecian god; thanksgiving to the tenders of the vine, that grew the grapes, that made this wine. May their shadow never lengthen to the east. (*All drink.*)

Ludovico.—Fill up again, it gives me thirst for more, sets my blood on fire, gives a generous warmth, an all-pervading glow, and moves my sluggish heart.

Farota.—It makes the poor man rich—the rich man poor—turns the world, and all its people upside down; our cares sit lightly on our hearts; it dulls the edge of keen desire.

Leoni.—It steals our sense, imprisons our lofty souls, and weakens God's precious gift—the intellect.

Bertrand.—Desolate homes, aged gray hairs, and suffering hearts, a mother's saintly love—these and many more its heritage.

Bernado.—Come, come, we are too hard on wine—generous wine. The fault is in ourselves. Let us one and all drink to Signio's health and prosperity.

Bertrand.—Here is to the hostler of St. Marco's Square—always ready with wine, and game, to freshen the lagging hours—a short life, and a merry one for me. (All drink and say Signio forever.)

Ludovico.—Well, who can give us news? Has good old Venice gone to sleep?

Leoni.—You have heard the last decree of State—an extra tax upon the Jews. Some revenue to raise until the next one's due.

Bertrand.—Our council seem to be bad managers; the money gone already, and for what? We have naught to show; the same old housing we have seen since we were boys; we have no extra shipping that I see; no marble palaces as monuments of Venetian glory; St. Marco's Square's the same; the rialto shows no improvement. Where, I say, where, has the seven million ducats gone? Who can answer?

Leoni.—True, most true; where does the money go? Our ships they ride at anchor in every port, our commerce is the world's; the revenues immense. Where can these moneys go?

Ludovico.—A tax upon the Jews? Ha, ha, ha! They are the treasurers for the State; the money well in hand, they seem to thrive and save; will make it back again, from all our gay young nobles; we will make it from the poor; a little doubling of their precious backs, increase our golden store; the rate of interest, will be raised, among the moneyed Jews.

Bertrand.—It cannot last; the tension is too great---the string will break. One more turn, of the little screw, then good-bye council ten.

Alfonso.—Art mad; you know not what you say. The council, and the Doge's spies are everywhere, and thick as the busy little bees—not to extract honey, from the sweet, sweet flowers—but the truth, and in a manner, you least would like.

Bertrand—And must the seal of silence, be placed upon our lips—no liberty of speech, to censure, the conduct of our ducal council. Where, does the money go, I ask? Who can answer? Can we not change them, once a year? Why do we keep them? Because the nobles fear to loose, their iron grip upon the toilers of the sea.

Alfonso.—The Doge, can answer you, I ween; his answer would bring sorrow to your soul. Who are you, anyway, Antonio's son, the poor old fisherman?. It is by noble grace you are here; art friendly to the poor, and well you may be so; you are the poorest of the poor; you cannot go with us, and defend the other side.

Bertrand.—Wine, women and game, make equals of us here, at least. The time will come, when all things will be more equal, outside; (All start up say: What say you?) Be calm, gentlemen—when we are dead, oh! ah!! oh!! ah!!!

Alfonso.—I thought some deep-laid plot, was in your fertile brain.

Bertrand.—I hear more than you know of. The bone and sinew of the land, they think; can your worthy Doge stop that?

Alfonso.—With all ease. The headsman's ax can soon do that; a poniard thrust, poison---a thousand ways, Bertrand.

Bertrand.—The murmur of the poor, like the Adriatic sea —is vast—a little wind would reap the whirlwind.

Ludovico.—What mean you?

Bertrand.—The people's curses, though deep, are long. Mark you well; I say not there is high treason, hatching in low places, for it is not so; the people are most true, and loyal; the situation is not secure: one little spark would kindle a conflagration, that all the power of church, and State, could not repress.

Signio.—Away with politics; let's have more wine; why trouble, with affairs of State—leave them to older heads.

Ludovico.—Guido's daughter, is fair indeed—the fairest in all Venice. Only by chance we met this Venus. Guido was displeased, as one well could see; he guards her as close as any miser does his gold. Many a time, and oft, we wined and dined, beneath his humble roof; never yet have we laid eyes upon her, and never dreamed, one so fair, dwelt in those quaint old walls.

Signio.—Fairest of the fair, as thou well hast said, and if her heart's as stern, and unrelenting, as her noble sire's, she will be a match for all.

Ludovico.—Alfonso's fair and flattering speech, fell flat upon those dainty ears, and made no more impression, than a rapier thrust, upon a marble wall.

Alfonso.—I would have said more; I liked not Guido's scowling face—he seemed ill at ease. I'd rather rouse the tiger from his lair, than offend this Guido in the least.

Bertrand.—Your life were not worth the hazard of a die —a spitted hare would be as much.

Alfonso,—I know it well, and therefore am prepared by stealth, or otherwise, to win this lady fair: she seemed most pleased with me, and if I am a judge, those tell-tale eyes, and blushing cheeks, betrayed the love, her face could not conceal. I'll lay siege to her heart at once; a hundred ducats, that I win.

Ludovico.—She will be a target, for more shafts than thine; a prize so fair, will well be worth the winning. How will fair Mario feel, whose heart, you have already won? How will she take this slight? Beware, Alfonso, a woman scorned, breathes vengeance on the scorner, and like *Circe*, changes them to swine.

Alfonso.—One would well think, you had some claims yourself, and threw the gauntlet at my feet.

Ludovico.—The fight, is a fair one. I'll break a lance with thee. In the list, the victor wins my lady's favor, it may be you, or it may be me.

Alfonso.—A hundred ducats that I win; who will take my wager then? She will fall an easy prey—the falcon's swoop, will not be more sure. She is a novice, in the world's bad ways—truth to her is on every lip—no guile in human heart.

Bertrand.—The eagle soars above the hawk, and one fell swoop, upon this dove so fair, would rend the falcon limb from limb. A fig, for such a narrow soul as thine, Alfonso, so pure a heart. deserves a better fate.

[Enter two strangers. Seat themselves at a distant table and converse.]

Guido.—I knew, we would find him here. I promised Antonio, and the promise shall be kept. I like not the crowd, at yonder table, flushed with wine. There sits Bertrand, too.

Faroto.—Who comes so late? Some gallants, from some ladies fair.

Signio.—Waiters! wine for those gentlemen, at once.

Alfonso.—I'll make the race. A hundred ducats that I win the prize.

Signio.—I double it, thou dost not. If I am any judge of human nature, you will have no easy conquest.

Alfonso.—Guido's daughter shall be mine.

Guido.—By all the gods, they are speaking of my child.

Zeno.—Be calm my friend, be calm. 'Tis Alfonso and his mates, by all that's good.

Guido.—Villains!! Such profane lips, to speak of things so pure.

Zeno.—Come, Guido, away. Oh, unpropitious fate! Why came we here? Be calm, my brain, for thy very wit's sake.

Guido.—I'll stay, till Venice sinks beneath the sea. Silence! Listen, Zeno, listen!

Alfonso.—By fair means, or by foul, I care not which, her charms shall yield, to my seductive tongue. Fill up your goblets to the brim; we will drain them and refill. Seven times seven, to Guido's daughter: fit subject, for Juno's jealous wrath. The peer of Trojan Helen.

Guido.—(Springs forward, just as they raise to drink; knocks Alfonso's glass from his hands; falls to the floor; all spring back aghast.)
By all the furies, of Pluto's dark realm, the cup that's drained, shall be the last. (All set their glasses down.)

Alfonso.—Guido, by all the shades of death!

Guido.—Well, may your wine-flushed face turn pale Fools! idiots! degraded bestial things! with no more honor than the dogs. No braver hearts, than to defame some poor girl's name. I spit upon you, as too base to live, too damned to die.

Alfonso.—Take back your words, or we will pin you to the wall. (All draw and advance.)

Guido.—White livered cowards, advance! My nerves are steel, and true as this good blade. My blood is up, and surges through my veins. I am ready. Come, advance, brave men, advance. Zeno and I stand side by side.

Signio.—Waiters, one and all, down with Guido! Down with these base intruders! (All advance. Guido blows a whistle. Ten men in masks enter; place themselves by Guido's side, with drawn swords.)
(Tableaux.) Curtain falls. End of first act.

SCENE.—[In Guido's Garden.—Enter Zelia and Silvia.]

Zelia.—How strange the sight, of Alfonso's face, should dwell so in my heart. Handsome, and proud of main, with all the ease, and bearing of a nobleman. His flattering speeches, would turn an older head than mine. How strange my father should have been so much disturbed, by my unexpected entrance. Does he hope to keep me, a close prisoner? Will some nun's cloistered life be mine, or will I always (in his eyes) be a child, and treated as one? Can you answer, Silvia?

Silvia.—I can, my child. Your best of fathers, has so ordered, that you can go at will—your happiness his only wish.

Zelia.—Oh, noble sire! How can I thank you, enough for this? Thrice noble, thou. Tell me all, what said he, Silvia.

Silvia.—Said you could go, and come at will: gave me the money for your dresses, laces, and fine jewels; and bade me spare him no expense—'twas for his darling child.

Zelia.—Thrice happy heart. To think I'll be a lady grand. How many pages shall I own, to bear this royal train? I have all a woman's heart could wish for, excepting, one little thing, and this I quite forgot.

Silvia.—What is it, child. It shall be yours.

Zelia.—Alfonso's love and admiration, when his handsome eyes, looked into mine, he read the secret of my heart

Silvia.—This I cannot promise, my child.

Zelia—I have changed my mind, good Silvia. I care not to go, beyond these garden walls ; I'll stay at home.

Silvia.—What mean you child, and why this change? You are jesting with me now.

Silvia.—Your eager wish, to mingle. with these courtly Venetian dames—and shine a peerless star, with wealth enough to buy a throne. You tell me now, you care not to go?

Zelia.—Reprove me not, good nurse; for that, I cannot help. I have a woman's heart within me.

Silvia.—What mean you?

Zelia.—Man's transgression through a woman came. The forbidden fruit, was sweetest to the taste. Say not the father's so.

Silvia.—Because you are allowed, full freedom from all restraint, you care not now to mingle with the throng.

Zelia.—You have well said.

Silvia.—Your father will rejoice, at this turn of your mind. I will restore this gold at once.

Zelia.—Hold, Silvia; be not so fast. I may yet, change my mind. I would give this all, for one little corner in Alfonso's heart. Will these fair gallants, call soon? and when? Would they were here now. You are so stupid, Silvia. I tire of thee, which liked you the best.

Silvia.—None my child, for the selfsame reason, was your noble sire so much chagrined.

Zelia.—And why? Oh, tell me why.

Silvia.—They are a heartless set. The best impulses of their lives, reach no higher than a broken heart, or empty flagon. Of this they boast.

Zelia.—What do you mean?

Silvia.—They would win your love, and honor too, for a base, ignoble use. There! I can say no more. If your father could find, some brave young heart, untainted by this worldly world, and all its wicked ways. he would be proud to own him for a son—where will he find as much, and in Venice, too.

Zelia.—How knows he, that my love would follow, in his train of thought? Remember well, I am but a child. The forbidden fruit, is sweetest to my taste. Alas, for human nature!

Silvia.—It grieves me, Zelia, to hear all this. Gray hairs, and declining age, give us ripe experience. You do but jest, to worry this old heart. You are a wayward child at best.

Zelia.—A ducat for your tame young man, with Monkish-praying ways. I like the reckless dash, of these gay Venetian gallants, as sparkling, as the wine they drink. Would I were a man, I'd live a thousand years in one.

Silvia.—Ah! my poor Zelia; you are the dazed moth, whose golden wings, will soon be singed, by the meridian glare, that blinds, yet burns. Let Phaeton's fate, serve thee as a warning. You ask for a most fatal gift. Be warned in time.

Zelia.—I do not understand.

Silvia.—You will when naught is left, but those poor singed wings. As your father well has said, take not the shadow for the substance.

[Enter Page, with note from Alfonso.

Page.—Lady most fair, I have instructions, from my noble young master, to place this in your hands, and in yours alone. You are the lady I seek—my good eyes tell me as much. I could not well go wrong: the description was good indeed—and while you read, I'll wander through this lovely spot, and wait your answer.

Zelia.—Oh, happy heart. This new-born love—the very dawn of life. My soul's entranced. (Opens and reads.) His pen's as ready as his tongue. Sweet breathings of love— I press thee to my heart. He fears, that I will offended be, at this bold avowal of his love. Oh, Alfonso! you know not Zelia's heart. Quick! some one—Silvia, pen and ink at once.

Silvia.—Hold, my child. You must be crazed, and need the leeches care. You'll answer no note of his. Let me see the letter. (Holds out her hand.)

Zelia.—No eyes but mine will ever see this note. I am no child. Good Page!——

Page.—At your service, lady.

Zelia.—Tell him, I'll send an answer soon—and now depart.

Silvia.—I have not yet seen that note, my child. Will you not show it to me?

Zelia.—Do not ask this of me. The note is to myself alone and is not for other's eyes. You would laugh good, Silvia.

Silvia.—Far from it, child. I'd sooner cry—too serious, to be the subject of a senseless jest. Your first downward step is taken—the road is sure and swift. The first lesson of life, you have learned, and that is deceit. Go, tell your father all; keep nothing back. You are withholding the truth, from those who love you most—whose every wish is for your happiness, and peace of mind.

Zelia.—Go, good Silvia; get thee hence, and leave me in peace.

Silvia.—Poor wayward heart. Leave thee in peace! I would that it could be so. There is no peace for thee. Cupid's arrow was well aimed—the shaft sunk deep. The wound's incurable. I tell thee now, thy father's good will, is wanting in this suit, and always will be. He would stop at nothing, to prevent thy downward fall. I'll to thy sire and tell him all.

Zelia.—I am alone—thank God for that—and can commune with my own thoughts. I'll analyze this froward heart

—this priceless love; and can Alfonso's love be mine?—the
first avowal of my life, and from so grand a king! Would
that I could see him now, and tell him of my love. This
would never do. We have met but once. Is this all
right, or wrong? I should ask advice of those who love
me most. Who loves me most, my lover, or my sire. Poor
heart, how can you well decide, between the two? I was too
impulsive. I'll not write the note. If he loves me, he will
send, or call, again. My reason tells me, the too ripe fruit
falls soonest, and soonest decays, and cloys the appetite.
Keep him on the hook, of keen desire, man soon tires of tame
possession, of the thing, he once did love. I have my father's
solid brain. I'll see how deep his love for me will be—not
too hasty, Zelia—wait, wait. [Exit.]

SCENE.—[In Guido's room.—Enter Silvia.]

Guido.—What ails thee, Silvia; you look care-worn and
pale. Speak; is my child ill?

Silvia.—No; in perfect health of person, though her heart's
diseased. Alfonso's page, came through the garden gate,
close by the marble pier. How he entered unannounced, I
know not. Before we well could speak, he was upon us,
with a love-note, which he straight did place in Zelia's hand.
She, in raptures of delight, reads it o'er and o'er, and presses
to her heart. His evil eye, has fallen upon her—Alfonso's
won her pure young heart, and she—she loves him madly.

Guido.—A thousand curses, on this hell-born hound. I'll
run him through, with this good sword of mine, before my
child should wed, so mean, and base a thing. I'll send her
soul to God while pure—her body to the Adriatic sea. Good
Silvia, be well on your guard. Watch every move; we will
circumvent this ungodly knave.

Silvia.—I'll need some help to watch, the garden gate, and
intercept these love-ladened notes, and guard the garden
wall.

Guido.—All that you can wish for, or want, and money too,
for that. [Exit Silvia.]

Dive deep into this fertile brain, and bring forth a god like
Minerva, fully armed, and panoplied for war. The gage of
battle, has been thrown at my very feet. Between thee and
me, Alfonso, a gulf of hate, so wide extends, a thousand pure
and white-robed angels, could never pass between. My
battle-flag floats proudly o'er my head, black as the raven's
wing, with crossed bones and skull. It bodes little good for
thee, since the gods so will it, that I have no peace at home;
and from this paradise, be driven forth, since plot, is to be,
met, by counterplot. I'll give them enough, till they cry quit.
Oh, for some quiet, sylvan shade, far removed from a city's
sinful ways. What brought my wandering footsteps, to this
quaint old town? Since I am here, why here I'll stay, till
shadowy-winged death, shall fall upon my soul. Rise, proud

ambition, and like a sparkling diadem, sit on this brow. I choose to be the Doge of Venice. The people, bowed down by tax, and poverty, are ripe and ready for a change. Give them a Republic indeed, and not in name. From distant time, a handful of liberty-loving fishermen, came to these scattering isles, and here forgotten by the potentates of earth, they founded the first republic of the world. The people ruled for ages, down to the present time, until by ballot the much dreaded ten, now rule this marbled city of slaves. The Republic is no more. I have more money, than the Duke himself. I'll use it well—buy up their spies—an easy task, since they already growl; and like some famished wolf, show their white teeth. They have not been paid for months— the longest purse wins with most ease. The Doge is cruel, as relentless fate. The Duke is good at heart, and is basely de- ceived by this thieving Doge, whose vaulted coffers, run over with ill-gotten gains. He has robbed the state, these many years; for what purpose, who can tell? I work secure, for under the crusader's flag, they dare not harm one hair. The church of Rome will bless me, and bring safety to my cause. Down with the Doge and ten—up with Guido, and the Re- public !

Zeno.--Are you dreaming, man. I have been at the door, this half hour or more.

Guido.—Your pardon, Zeno; I was lost in thought—paint- ing mind-pictures.

Zeno.—Painting mind-pictures? What mean you?

Guido.—A picture, that Liberty helps me paint—the god- dess I most adore.

Zeno.—Let me but glance upon it, I will be content.

Guido.—Thou canst not peer into this mind. The game of chess is set, pieces all in place. Who first cries mate?

Zeno.--You speak in oracles; I do not understand.

Guido.—He is wisest, who closest keeps his tongue.

Zeno.—I thought I was your friend.

Guido.—You may well believe me, when I say you are. As such, I love and reverence you. Here is my hand; be patient, the time has not come; be astonished at nothing, for you'll see Guido in strange places, at any and all times. Zeno, you have never met my daughter. You, of all Venice, are the only one, I'd trust, with this sweet child's happiness. I introduce you, as my friend—Guido's friend—and this is saying much. [Rings. Enter Page.] Bid your young mistress come at once. [Enter Zelia.] Zeno, this is my daughter. My daughter Zelia, this is my friend.

Zeno.—By the distant stars, I blame not Guido, for his dis- creet guard. You would turn the heads of Venice, with all ease.

Zelia.—My father's friend is mine, and always will be so. You are welcome to our hospitality.

Zeno.—I knew not you had a daughter grown, and must confess I was surprised.

Zelia.—You must indeed, be father's friend, for never yet, have these eyes of mine, beheld so strange a thing.

Zeno.—You go not out much then, and meet but few.

Zelia.—I am up with the lark—before Phœbus' prancing, neighing steed, their daily course begin. I breathe the early morning breeze, from off the Adriatic sea. 'Tis better than the nectar of the gods.

Zeno.—Thy very face, would tell as much. I fear me our Venetian beauties, stir not abroad so soon. Like all things else, the human face divine, requires the sun's bright ray, to bring color, to the cheek, and sparkling brightness, to the eye.

Zelia.—To be one of these belles, the very thing I dream most of. I hate restraint; it is a childish punishment. Had I mixed more with these Venetians, I would not now so wish, to be ever on the wing. I dream, and dream again, of all this pleasure seeking throng, until my foolish brain, is all in a whirl.

Guido.—Zelia, you shall drain pleasure's cup, to the very dregs. The prize, we most do seek, when in our possession, becomes a worthless thing. You will be disappointed, my child, my word for it. Are these painted dolls, with their constant round of pleasures, more happy than you? Believe it not. Zeno and I, are at your service, at any and all times, to counsel and protect.

Zelia.—Half the pleasure of your promise, is gone already. Freedom of thought and action, without restraint, to me, is liberty indeed.

Guido.—I am afraid to risk, your young and guileless heart; all is rottenness, and festering corruption here—the whited sepulchre, my child. Be ever on your guard—take not the shadow for the substance. Believe not half you hear. Sift well the truth—dissembling hearts, flattering tongues, masqued faces, are all you'll see, though covered by sweet smiles, and velvet clothes.

Zelia.—I am all eagerness. When shall we go? (Aside: Alfonso, to meet thee, is happiness enough.)

Zeno.—I shall be proud, to be the gallant knight of such a lady fair. 'Twere well worth a broken lance, to win a smile from such a lovely face, or crack a helmet for my lady's favor. Do you accept, fair Zelia?

Zelia.—I do, and thank you too. You over-rate the service much.

Guido.—We will say good-night. How can I tell thee, of a father's anxious heart? Never forget, your poor old faithful sire; his teachings, and his tender care. May all the saints, in Rome's calendar, preserve thee from this danger. [Exit Guido and Zeno.

Zelia.—I know what father means—can tell his inmost

thought. He hopes by Zeno, to divert my mind, from my
Alfonso; make me forget, this first love of my life. Never!
You little know me, my father. They say, Alfonso's false—
his love as fleeting as the summer wind. I'll see for myself,
and should he prove untrue, my love would turn to hate so
deep, 'twould sink him fathoms, in Pluto's dark domains. To
meet Alfonso, the thought is rapture, to my wayward heart.
Dream on, and may you never know dispair, the agony of a
broken heart.

SCENE.—[In Guido's office.]

Guido.—[Rings for a page—Enters.] Call all my men
from work—the day is done. Bid them come to the office;
I have some words for each, and money too.

Bruno.—We are all here, good master, and would know
thy smallest wish.

Guido.—Bruno, see that the doors, and windows, are well
barred, and bolted too, and that no one lingers near. I have
much to say, and only for your faithful ears, my men.

Bruno.—'Tis done, and well done too. We are ready, and
all attention.

Guido.—We have worked long together, and I well could
swear, to trust thee with my life, and feel it safe in your good
keeping. Speak! Is it not true?

Bruno—Long live Guido! It is the solemn truth.

Zuido.—Have I not made your happiness, my constant
study?

Men.—You have.

Guido.—I want your help. A plot to overthrow this
tyrant Doge, and his base minions, lurkes within my fertile
brain, and only needs your stout hands, and stouter hearts, to
carry to fruition. Will you, one and all, stand by me, in this
scheme?

Men.—We will.

Bruno.—Do you count the cost, good master? Are you
not afraid of the Doge's spies? Lion of St. Mark, death,
and torture on the rack, if you should fail. What would become of us—our occupation gone? We would be paupers in
Venice.

Guido.—Dread nothing; fear nothing. Guido is at the
helm. The old Venetian ship, will sail so straight, on her
good way, we will be in port, before the storm-king's loose.
We will work, while others sleep—be companions for the owl.
The blow will fall so suddenly, they will not have time to
think. You came promptly at my call, when I was sore
beset, by those gambling knaves, on St. Marco's Square.
The Duke is kind of heart, and loves not such cruel torture.
He is himself, ruled by this thieving Doge. Down with the
Doge, I say. Your fathers, and grand-fathers, can well remember, when Venice was free; the people ruled, and woe to
the Duke, or Doge, who sought to overthrow the people's

will, as you well know, the oppressor's yoke, is on our necks.
No baser slaves gaze on the rising sun. Is there no brave
hearts, in Venice to-day? or has the inquisition, with their
dreaded torture, paled the fires of liberty, that burned so
brightly, for your sires, and mine? Stand by me, my men:
rekindle those sacred fires. We will bring peace and plenty.
to this ancient town. This Doge is stealing from the State:
his vaults are filled with golden ducats, wrenched from the
hands of toil—these idle aristocrats—they bring no wealth to
Venice; they uphold this council of ten, because it brings
them safety from all danger. They can sleep in peace, while
poor seafaring men are robbed. Equal tax for all, equal
rights for all, protection to the humblest in the land.

Bruno.—Well done, good master ; our aid, you shall have.
though it cost, us our lives.

Guido.—W'ell, swear, and bind thee by a solemn oath.

All.—We will.

Guido.—Then all kneel down; out with your daggers.
crossed handles up, and follow me. By this red cross I
swear, by the blood in our veins, by the cross of our dagger's
hilt, by the hopes of our eternal lives, by the shadow of
gloom and of death, by the grave, and its secrets well kept ;
we swear to be true, and be brave, and the cord, and the
dagger, for him, who betrays, and so, we solemnly swear; all
kiss the cross. Arise, we are a band of brothers. I name
thee, Knights of the Red Cross. And now with my plans:
with the cunning of the fox, we will add the courage of the
lion; we must buy their spies with gold, which will be easy
done. A set of shiftless knaves, who would serve the devil
for a song—approach them cautiously, and not in haste, for
this of all requires your greatest tact. A glass of wine—gain
their confidence ; shake well filled purses in their faces—the
thing is done. I wish them not, to leave the Doge's service ;
this would ruin all our plans. draw pay from both, the
secrets of the council, will be ours, and they will know nothing, of our plans—all the advantage will be ours. I'll get the
name of every spy. They must never be admitted to our
council. The Doge's secretary, will give me these names.
Divide Venice into districts, and each one work his field ; it
will not look well, to meet in one place, so large a gathering would not escape, the Doge's evil eyes. Tell these good
people, of their wrongs, our object, and our plans; select
some secret places; get thee thither, one by one; work silently,
and well, prescribe this oath you have just taken; tell them
who their leader is, and also that we can work in safety, for
a crusade to the holy land, will disarm suspicion. I will attend to this—see these good fathers, and by the powerful aid
of Rome, we will be protected, in our scheme. Meet here
two weeks hence; at this self same hour, and remember well.
Guido's life is in thy hands. [Exit men.] My plans work

well. I'll at once to these good fathers, and lay before them, my crusader's plans—ask their blessing, and protection on our good work. This will disarm suspicion, from the powers that be—the church upon my side, the power of Rome is all supreme; they make, and unmake kings, at will.

SCENE—[In Alfonso's house. Enter Page.]

Alfonso.—Well, good Page, the answer to my note, from Guido's daughter.

Page.—I have no note; she bade me tell thee, she would send one soon.

Alfonso—How received she the note?

Page.—In ecstasy, she read it o'er and o'er, devoured every word and line, and like a famished wolf, she picked the bones, pressed it to her heart, kissed and fondled it as some precious thing. (I wish I was that note.)

Alfonso.—Out upon thee for a knave, and was it not to her, some precious thing?

Page.—I have gone so often, on such love-ladened errands. and so oft, have seen the self-same scene, I long ago have felt, your love is no precious thing. (Rather promiscuous.)

Alfonso.—Insolent; I'll lay this good blade well on your back.

Page.—At the same time, good master, I wish you'd lay some past due wages, in my purse. Where is fair Mario, whose form, and face divine. charmed your fickle soul awhile? Have you thrown her off, as some old glove?

Alfonso.—It matters not to thee. I have not seen her these three good months. I would tire of an angel in a week.

Page.—Where is Lucretia, then?—a stately dame, as ever trod the marbled paves, of proud old Venice, a very queen of most royal bearing; 'twas long the citadel of her heart, withstood thy heartless siege and yielding all, gave heart and soul to thee.

Alfonso.—Don't call up these forbidden ghosts, of former times, they make me feel uncomfortably.

Page.—Mario, will not let thee off so light; one false step, will bring a thousand more. When she finds, you love her no longer, and even now, dote on this Guido's daughter, her four brothers, will make short work of thee. Then Guido, as fierce as any buccaneer, who sails the Adriatic sea; how will you parry his rapier thrust? A foot of shining steel, through thy loving heart, would soon tire, the angels of thee —(I mean fallen ones.)

Alfonso.—'Tis at my risk, not thine. I'll be the scabbard that receives the blade—my blood, not yours will flow.

Page.—Good master, before all this happens, I'd like to have my pay; many days have passed, since I received one ducat, from thee. Signio, the friend of thy bosom, makes sport of thy fat purse. Wins all thy wealth—drugs thy very wine, for ought I know, and then good-by ducats, and Alfonso's luck.

Alfonso.— You have been a faithful Page, and prompt to do my bidding; other Pages fare no better; all the glitter, and the show, for the outside world, stint, and poverty, at home, a breakfast, on a crust of bread, a drink of stale, bad wine, that we may amble forth in gay attire, and people call us rich.

Page.—Give me my dues, good master, and I leave. Rats desert a sinking ship.

Alfonso.—I have it, not, to give; my luck has forsaken me, at present. It will return; I'll borrow from the Jews—pawn my diamonds. I cannot let thee go.

Page.—Say one week hence. I'll give thee that much time.

Ludovico—Good morrow; you look worried and pale; what goes wrong with thee?

Alfonso.—Everything, Ludovico, everything. I have no luck at cards ; my servants cry for pay, and will not be quiet. Should they all leave at once, not a corner in all Venice, but would hear the cause; the masque would drop, my creditors, would seize everything. Harrassed by debt, I know not what to do.

Ludovico.—Marry some rich girl. She will mend thy broken lance: give thee another tilt, with the ever-fickle goddess—dame fortune.

Alfonso.—I distrust these rich girls much, perhaps like my good self, they exist only, for the outside world—poverty at home. Who knows, they are rich; the people so say, and do the people know? They have rich ways, that's all.

Ludovico.—One half the world, lives on the other half, and will be so, for all time to come. Keep up your dress, and above all, your sweet address. If that smooth tongue of thine, wins not a wealthy bride, I am done. Where shall we meet to-night?

Alfonso.—Any place, you say, will suit me. Oh! for some good, good wine, to drive away, these wretched thoughts. The ducal ball comes off, a few days hence, I must prepare. I'll meet you at any place, to-night.

Ludovico.—This ducal ball, will be grand, indeed; all Venice will be there, and well she may, for Venice pays the payer. Meet us at Signio's to-night, and better luck, next time. [Exit both.]

Guido—[Scene in the old Cathedral.] (Enter.)

A solemn awe, steals round my heart, in this holy place; those sculptured saints, call back forbidden thoughts. We all must die, and lie forgotten in the gloom of death. All prepare to live—few prepare to die. Mad ambition, crowds out these heavenly thoughts—the world moves on. I'll to the Monkish quarters in the rear (music plays), their solemn chants break faintly on my ear. I'll follow the sound. [Knocks. Some one within says enter. Scene changes; room in monastery—Monks in place.]

Francisco—First Monk.—What, would you have my son? The peace, the world, can never give.

Guido.—Thy blessing, good father, then I'll speak of that. which brought me here.

First Monk.—You have our blessing; speak, for life is all too short—eternity before us, and never ending. Time itself shall be no more.

Guido.—You know my calling, do you not? I am a dealer, in that which kills the body, and sets the spirit free, to find eternity—the armorer---Guido by name.

First Monk.—Your name is well known, within these walls. My son---not for thy worldly trade---but, for the good deeds you have done. I like not your calling; 'tis a brutish one. Life is sweet to all---even to the lowest of God's creation. Why take this precious life?

Guido--Most true, good father, but for these same good blades, that let the life's blood out, thy heavenly calling, were not worth a fig. Men think not of death, till this dark angel, fans our fleeting breath. 'Tis yours, to smooth the rugged path of life, to make us more content, with what we have, sooth sorrowing hearts, and when the eye is glazed in death, to fold our hands across, our storm-tossed breasts, and pray for the departing soul.

First Monk.—So thou sayest, my son, and by my faith, it is all wrong, that God's created things should suffer so. Think of the valiant hearts, that face the foeman's steel, and as the waving ranks sink down, all trampled, in the gloom of agony and death, can man be God's own image, and shed blood so?

Guido.—We prepare them, for their Godly calling; 'tis doubly sweet, to smooth the pillow of the dying---bind up the shattered limb, and lave the fevered lip.

First Monk.—We will speak no more of this, it makes my blood run cold, to think man's such a cruel thing.

Guido---One question more, and I am done: What think you of these goodly knights, who risk their lives, to regain the Savior's tomb?

First Monk.---The prayers of the church, are with them, my son, for 'tis a holy cause, and one most just.

Guido.---Do they not need good swords, and true, corselet, helmet, battle-ax, and spear, to crush these unbelieving Turks?

First Monk---"Tis in the service of the Lord, and therefore, just. God commands, and we obey.

Guido.---Then, to my business, at once. It is my wish, to lead an army of brave knights, from proud old Venice. For very truth's sake, it is a shame, that we have lagged so long, in this good cause.

First Monk.---God will bless you for this, my son; death, would be sweet in such a cause.

Guido.—Your counsel, I would seek, good father—as you well know; 'tis fraught with danger, in Venice. Our worthy Doge, by ducal decrees, permits not the assembling of so great a throng---no secret meetings, 'tis at the peril of my life. How am I to proceed, in this good cause?

First Monk—We will study up, some plan.

Guido.—Could you not obtain the Pope's permission, and good will---safety to my person, and my men, a decree protecting us from the Doge's spies, and torture? I could then work, with hands untied. As it is, a dungeon, or the block, would be my sure reward.

First Monk.—Never! while the Church of Rome is free ! It shall be as you wish. Our good father, the Pope, will uphold your cause; and who will dare, to harm one hair? The curse of Rome will surely fall, on King, Baron, Dodge, or Duke. I will despatch a messenger, this very night, and have the papers here, one week hence. I am proud to think so brave a heart, dwells in sin-polluted Venice.

Guido.—How can I thank you, enough, good father, for your priestly offices, in my behalf? And, now, to work. When will the papers come? When shall I call?

First Monk.—Say one week, hence. I'll post a messenger, this very night.

Guido.—I crave pardon, good fathers, that I did disturb your solemn services. And now, farewell. [Exit.]

[SCENE—changes to the Cathedral aisle.]

Guido.—Poor, humane hearts, that weep, for very woe, because blood flows, and, men are killed! They bless the cause, that sweeps them off, by thousands, in this holy war. They seize, by force, that, which, belongs not to them. The sad, sad, heart, of some fair maid, who waves a long farewell. from some old castle wall; mothers, and sons, with streaming eyes, fond, and, may be, last embraces; brave hearts, in casques of steel—and, with their waving plumes, ride on, to death, through leagues of sea, and land, to right a childish wrong, an empty dream—not worth a single thought, though, it serves my purpose, well—gods! how good thou art. A rupture, between Church, and State; and, with the papal decree, in my possession, I am safe. Can hurl defiance, in their very teeth. There are older heads, than thine, good Guido, but, none, more fertile to conspire.

[SCENE:—In Guido's garden. Alfonso climbs over the garden wall, followed by page.]

Alfonso.—Softly, good page, softly! We tread on dangerous ground. Should we be discovered, here, Guido, and his brawny crew, would make short work. Are the ladders, in place, and ready, for retreat? Too much risk, by half. Know you, the situation here?

Page.—While waiting, for the note, I used my eyes, to some good purpose. This way, my master, this way.

Alfonso.—Would, that I could meet, this charmer here!
'Tis a secluded spot, and, suits well my plans.

Page.—Wait, here; I'll forward, and see if all is quiet. I
know the bearings, well.

Zelia.—I hear voices; though, it cannot be. Who, should
be here, at this hour, but Silvia and myself? Even Silvia,
has gone, within. I am alone. It sounded, to my ears, like
brave Alfonso's. Oh, would, that he were here! I cannot tear
his image, from my heart; he is with me, in my dreams. And
father says, he is a villain. Can this be true? My father
must be prejudiced; perchance, he wrongs a noble soul.

Page—Lady, your pardon!

Zelia.—What do you here! You came not, through the garden gate. Speak! I'll call my father.

Page.—Softly, my lady; not so much haste. Alfonso's
near at hand, and all impatience. Will you see him?
Then, follow me.

Zelia--How know you, that I care to meet Alfonso?

Page—My eyes and ears, tell me as much. Did I not see
thee, when you received his note? Did I not hear, those
sweet, sweet, words, of love, but a moment since ?

Zelia.—You are a presumptuous page. Lead on; I'll follow. Be still, my poor, poor, heart; you will break all
bounds! To meet Alfonso; the thought is rapture! There
is no harm, in this. What will he think ; what would my
father say ?

Alfonso.—Zelia! The gods be praised, for this. It is a risk
to meet thee, here : the recompense, is adequate.

Zelia.—I do wrong, to meet you, in this secluded place; it
is not maidenly, or right.

Alfonso.—The risk, is mine. Should this good sire, of
thine, find me, in this place, my life, were not worth the
saving.

Zelia.—Then, why did you come?

Alfonso.—The reason, stands before me, and a fair one, too.

Zelia.—Your tongue's, as ready as your sword.

Alfonso.—Can we not think, of some good place, where
we could meet, in secret—be more at ease? Every moment's, filled with danger, here.

Zelia.—I'll meet you at the Ducal ball.

Alfonso.—Oh, rapture! And you, will be there ? My happiness will be complete. How will I know you, fair
Zelia ?

Zelia.—By the rosette, on my hat—black, red and blue—
pinned with a silver arrow.

Alfonso.—How can we part, so soon; and, yet, it must be
so. Farewell! I'll count the very hours, 'till we meet again.
[Exit, Alfonso and Zelia.]

Portio.—Ha! ha! ha! Walls have ears, and so has Portio,
too. My new found master, will pay me well, for this. Al-

fonso, I hate you, with a devil's hate. You struck me once.
Portio never forgets. You killed my only sister, too. I have
waited long; my time has come! I'll shadow thee, with
sleepless eyes; you shall not escape me now! I am well paid,
by Guido, whom I love. Gold, with my revenge; 'tis good
enough. I'll to Guido at once. [Knocks at Guido's door;
scene changes.]

Guido.—Enter! What have you, to report? I am waiting, Portio,

Portio.—Much, good master, much. I was on the watch,
within the garden ; a ladder was placed against the wall.
Who should descend, but Alfonso, and his page! By my
faith! had you been there, they would have died with fright.
They picked their way most cautiously. Alfonso halted, the
page advanced, and found your daughter, alone. They met,
parted; to meet again, at the Ducal ball. They recognize
each other, by a rosette of black, red, and blue, surmounted
with a silver arrow, placed upon her hat.

Guido.—I thank you, Portio; there is a ducat for thy vigilance. I will pay thee well. Never let this villain meet my
daughter. I have a note to send : be ready, at once. Know
you, where fair Mario lives?

Portio.—Right well, my master.

Guido.—I'll write at once. [Writes.] FAIR MARIO. Be
at the Ducal ball, and, for an unknown friend's sake, wear a
rosette, upon your hat, of black, red, and blue, pinned with
a silver arrow. This will prove Alfonso false to thee. Come,
without fail. Be silent, and hear what you will hear.---YOUR
FRIEND. Place this letter in her own hands ; watch and
wait. Never lose sight of Alfonso. Tell me how he
dresses ; also, the Doge, and his good scribe, without fail, for
'tis important to know.

Portio.---To hear, is to obey. Fear not: I'll trail him, till
you bid me halt. [Exit.]

Guido.---By all the furies, that dwell in darkened hell, I'll
wreck my vengeance on this brute. Calm down, black hate;
your time's not come! Oh! sorrow to my heart. To think
my only, darling child, is charmed, with this, cursed snake!
Heavy, already, are the sins, upon his head. Cursed,
doubly cursed, the day that called thee, into existence! Pay-
day, will come, at last ; and, what a day, for thee!

Guido.---What, Portio: back already? You must have
used Mercury's wings.

Portio.---All that you could wish. The Doge will dress
in a black, velvet suit; a large, white plume, will droop upon
his right shoulder ; the buckle of his sword belt will be of
solid gold, with a silver lion's head, in bold relief.

Guido.---It is enough. How will his scribe, and treasurer,
dress?

Portio.---A jester's suit, with tiny silver bells: sword belt, sky blue; with silver buckle, and huntsmen's horn attached.

Guido.---Well done, good Portio; how found you, all this out?

Portio.·· As good luck, would have it, the tailor, who made them, both, was my best of friends. I also delivered your note, to the lady, herself. She will be at the ball ; and, from her looks, the paleness, that o'erspread her face, bodes little good, for my hated foe.

Guido.—I thank thee, Portio; 'twas a lucky day for Guido, when I called, thee, to my service. Be brave, be true, and ever, on his track. Let not his smallest thought, escape thee. The time, will come, when you shall, be avenged, and have my gold, besides. Now go, and serve, me well. My deep laid plans, work well. I must prepare, myself a dress, and without the aid, of outside help. Too many spying eyes, would spoil, my cherished scheme. My broad-chested, brawny-armed men, bring me good news. Our ranks fill up, with the bone and sinew of the land. Well may this cursed Doge, doubt Guido's plan. His wolfish fangs, once drawn, by the church of Rome, he can only, like some whipt cur, stand back, and growl. I'll call Silvia, at once.]Rings. Enter Page.] Tell Silvia, I wish, her presence, at once.

Silvia.—What would you, good master.

Guido.—I want your help.

Silvia.—'Tis yours, to order.

Guido.—I want a costume, for the ducal ball. What shall it be? 'Twere best, to represent Mephistopheles. Can you have it ready, in time? Zelia must not know, of this. Tell no one, and be prompt.

Silvia.—It shall be done. About Zelia?

Guido.—Zelia must not go—would spoil my work. Let her get all things in readiness, and when she sups, pour this sleeping solution in her wine. 'Tis tasteless, and will do no harm. She will feel no pain. Sleep well, my child, it is to, save thee, from a living death. She will not wake, until the sun, with fiery steeds, has half his journey run.

Silvia.—'Tis for her good, and shall be well done.

SCENE.—[In Ducal Place and Garden adjacent.—Ball within.]

Guido.—'Tis cooler in this lovely place; I breathe more free. The air within, is stifling. I greatly fear me, they will not come. 'Tis late already; the rooms are filled, and yet, I see them not. Can Portio be false? I will not so believe. Revenge, is sweeter than my gold, to him. I see fair Mario pass this way, and with her four brothers, all in masque. I'll watch her close—by this means, will find Alfonso. I see him now; he presses through, this masquerading throng, and with such eager haste—is by her side, and whispers in her ear. They come this way—I'll step behind this tree.

Alfonso.—Fair Zelia, you have promised well; and better,

have fulfilled, the promise. I feared me much, you would not come.

Mario.—(In a low voice)—And you love me, as you say. Alfonso?

Alfonso.—Better, than my very life.

Mario.—You have loved others, as much, as you now, love me. I have heard, you once loved Mario; is it so?

Alfonso.—True, in every word, and line. I soon grew, weary of her love.

Mario.—How know I, you will not soon tire, of mine?

Alfonso.—By those eternal stars, that shine so steadfast, I pledge undying love to thee.

Mario.—Swear not, Alfonso, for thy oath's sake. A broken vow, is like a broken lance—'tis worthless, only to be thrown away. You hate this Mario then, and for my sake, will cast her image from thee?

Alfonso.—I swear to you, she is naught to me, and ever will be. I thought her rich, and found her poor—too poor to waste my heart upon.

Mario.—Perhaps, you thirst, for father's wealth, and love me but for this.

Alfonso.—When first we met, my heart, and eyes, were dazzled, by thy peerless beauty. Please unmask, but for a moment, and let my heart be gladdened by thy winsome smile.

Mario.—Be happy then, Alfonso. [Jerks off her mask. Alfonso stares, and staggers back a pace.]
You seem not so well pleased, Alfonso.

Alfonso.—Great gods! Oh!! what a dupe I have been— some devil's hand in this.

Mario.—What have you now, to say? That false, and flattering tongue, for once, is speechless.

Alfonso.—I have lost my sense, as well. How came you. with that strange rosette?

Mario.—You base, and worthless thing. I can call thee, by no other name. Why did you win my love? Why betray the heart, that loved you, so well? Why betray the sacred honor in your keeping, and send *me* soulless, to the great white throne? A thousand curses, on your guilty soul. May your waking hours, be haunted, by the soul you have lost; your sleep be broken, by the ghost, of murdered innocence. God curse you, with his vengeance. May you never know one happy hour, in all time to come—be cursed, as you have cursed me! with your worthless love.

Alfonso.—Hold!! Silence!! I'll curse, and kill you, too.

Mario.—You killed my soul; now kill my body too. Life is worthless to me—death a blessing. Strike!

Alfonso.—Curse you, I will. [Rushes upon her, dagger in hand. Guido springs upon him, and throws him to one side.]

Guido.—Assassin! Coward!! This is not the first time, you have done so base a deed.

Alfonso.—Who are you, in this devil's garb? You had some hand in this.

Guido.—God be thanked, I came in time, to save this lady's life.

Alfonso.—Who are you? I'll tear the mask from your satanic face.

Guido.—Now go; begone, you will never know. I know *thee* well; and silent as the fallen leaf, I have tracked, you in your wild career. You have done base deeds enough, to send thee to a dungeon deep; and thought no eyes but thine, did see those hell-born acts. Begone, vile wretch; out of my sight.

Come, fair Mario, the air grows damp, and chill. This is no place for thee. Danger lurkes, in every bush, and flower. We will go, within, and find your brothers; then you will be safe.

Mario.—Please tell me, who you are, kind stranger. You seem to know us all. A mask is no protection. [Exit.]

Alfonso.—Foiled, by heavens, and my secret's in this stranger's hands. I'll wait without, and when he comes, send this keen stiletto blade, deep into this plebeian's heart. [Exit.]

Guido.—[Returns.] And now for my other game. I'll soon run them down. The shot at random, went straight to the mark. The cowering wretch, will try the assassin's dagger. [Looks all around.] No lurking foe, the coast is clear. I'll wait the coming of the Doge. He comes, without.

Doge.—How pure and fresh—this air, brings vigor to my lungs, pent up in those close rooms. It is a gorgeous pageant, and worthy of the Duke

Guido.—And worthy of the Doge, as he seems well pleased. indeed.

Doge.—Devil! for as such you seem. How know you that I am the Doge?

Guido.—Oh, start not; I know you well. Sooner or later, you will belong to me. I can prove to thee, I know all things, past and present.

Doge.—Give me the proof.

Guido.—Down deep in mother earth, beneath your palace, in a darkened vault in brass-bound chests, you've heaped up piles of gold. How did you get this wealth? You stole it from the Duke, and state. See how your faltering limbs, do tremble, and refuse to go. A miser's soul is thine, when all is hushed and still, you hold sweet commune, with your god. Such souls are mine

Doge.—In heaven's name, do tell me, who you are. I am undone. Come to my palace, and we will take some wine. I will pay thee well, for silence.

Guido.—I want not your gold; fear naught from me, I am a stranger in Venice, and before to-morrow's sun, shall rise, will be many leagues away.

Doge.—God be praised for this; I breathe more free. What brought you here ?

Guido.—To see your far-famed balls.

Doge.—Come to my palace. Why hurry hence? A day would make no difference with thee.

Guido.—I leave Venice to-night.

Doge.—I will within. Good-bye then. [Aside.---I will see that you do not leave.]—Exit.

Guido.—And now for the last, and most important. This Scribe, good slave, good master, he comes this way, and now be ready.

Scribe.—I am tired, and 'tis time to go. I'll rest and then prepare, to leave

Guido.—Start not; or does the fear of evil deeds, bring thy future lot, too close, for happiness. You are the Doge's scribe and treasurer?

Scribe.—You are mistaken, Devil.

Guido.—Shall I whisper words, for other ears, that would condemn thee to a prison cell?

Scribe.—You are a boastful liar, and know nothing, of me, or mine.

Guido.—You have served your master well; have filled his vaults, with stolen wealth. I can lead thee, to this very vault. A slip, of paper, in the lion's mouth, would stop, thy thieving hand; thy master's, too.

Scribe.—Spare me, knowing all ; I am, at thy mercy, and humbly beg for safety. What would you, with me? You have a purpose? Speak.

Guido.—You have a paper, on your person. Give it me, and, my tongue's, as silent as the grave. A list, of your secret spies.

Scribe.—I thought, you would ask me, for gold. Here, it is, and welcome.

Guido.—Tell not, your master, of this meeting, and all will be well; you'll hear, no more, of me. I leave, Venice, to-night. [Exit Scribe.] My work, is well, and truly done, and, now, I must, be gone ; I want not, the day, to break, and, find me, here. First, of all, I'll throw, this monkish garb, around me. Fools, you will wait, some time; Guido, is too much, for thee. Your daggers, and your spies, will never kill, or track me, to my door. [Steps behind a bush, and dons the garb; steps out.] Solemn step, and slow: bowed head, and meditation, deep; and so, I'll pass unseen.

[End of second act; curtain falls.]

[Scene:—In Council Hall; all seated in place.]

Duke.—What business, of import, brings us to this hall?

Doge.—Our ever, faithful, spies, find nothing, worthy of report, except this Guido, and his crazy crowd of crusaders—

Duke.—Well, what of him? What has, he done, that's worthy of the Council ?

Doge.—He is working, night and day, to get his squadron, ready, for the march. Well, let him, go; we will, be well, rid of him. I, like him, not; too fearless, of tongue, and bearing high.

Duke.—By whose authority, is all this, done?

Doge.—I know not; shall we, summon him?

Duke.—Let it, be so, ordered.

Doge.—[Rings a bell.] Page, take this, note, at once, to Guido; and, tell him, the Duke, and Council, wait.

Page.—He is without.

Duke.—Admit him; and, stand thou, without.

Guido.—Most, noble Duke! As such, I salute you. What may be, your good commands? I am ready, to obey.

Duke.—Good Guido! We, have been, informed, that you, with intent good and noble, equip a cavalcade, of knights, and 'squires, for service, in the Holy Land. By whose authority, is all this done? Speak!

Guido.—By all the gods. That face! It haunts me! Who can he be? Or, 'tis some strange resemblance.

Duke.—Why do you start—turn pale? There's nothing, here, to harm, thee.

Guido.—I fear, not man, be he King, Duke, slave or beggar. Your face, recalls, a cherished brother's; that was all. Pardon, the interruption, noble Duke. My authority, comes from, the Church of Rome; and, under this broad papal seal, I am protected. I have, the privilege, of calling, any, and all men, who wish, to go. I have, a small army, all ready, and, eager, for the march. The knightly calling, and the cause, bring numbers, to my banner. Had I your Grace's permission, to hold, secret meetings, and, without trouble, to your laws, to organize—it would expedite, my plans.

Duke.—Well spoken, Guido. It would, have been better, to have, asked me, first. The Church of Rome, is, too much, the master, now. It should, not be so.

Guido.—I crave pardon. Being a holy war, I presumed, 'twas of, the Church's ordering.

Duke.—My subjects to be, butchered, for the Church of Rome?

Guido.——Your pardon, again; I did not know. If you so will, I'll return, this, papal decree, and use yours, instead.

Duke.—It makes, little difference, now. You have our gracious permission, and, so will instruct, our guards, and spies. You are at liberty to depart. [Page, shows him out. Exit.] Guido has gone. My heart, seems strangely drawn, towards him. Noble, brave fellow, that he is!

Doge.—Your Highness, like, all others, admires, and loves him, too. I say, beware! The day will come, when he will do, us harm. I, like him not. His eagle eye pierced into my very soul, and seemed, to read, my secret mind, as some

well-filled parchment, open and displayed—would that he
were gone, already; I'd breath more free.

Duke.—What other business, before our gracious presence,
and this good council? What, of my last decree? How
stands the record, with thee, scribe?

Doge.—Your Highness, my worthy scribe, will hand, thee,
a full statement, of all moneys, received and spent, up to this
time.

Duke.—Have our, worthy councilmen, been promptly paid?

First Council.—You may well, be sworn, in this respect.
We give, no cause, for just complaint. This, is the prime
law, of all, governing bodies.

Duke.—Have our guards, and spies, been paid, in full?

Doge.—We are somewhat, in arrears; though, we promise
much, and they, seem satisfied.

Duke.—What say, you all; is it, your wish, that Crusader
Guido, and his men, be allowed, to meet, in secret, and organize? What think you, of the Pope's decree?

Second Council.—Will it weaken, the revenues, of State?
If so, I am opposed. Pope, or no Pope; the Church of
Rome, should meddle not, in secular affairs. Let them unto
their spiritual work, attend. There are souls, enough, to save.

Third Council—Why should it, not weaken, our tax, per
capita? We have been, these many years, trying to see,
what else, there is, to tax. We tax, the people, for the very,
privilege of allowing, them to live. We tax them, for their
own amusement. We tax the Jews, because they, of all
others, are the most fruitful, source, of revenue. Any citizen
of Venice, who wishes, our permission, to undertake some
enterprise, must cross, our palms, with gold. I have, often
thought, the Church of Rome, should tribute, pay; be taxed,
or saving souls.

Duke.—If Guido, take not, too many men, I have, no great,
objection. We, will reap, the glory: and the Church, will
pay. Let it be, so ordered. The Lion of St. Mark : what
has he, to say? No silent accusations; no great conspirators
against the State! And does, the Bridge of Sighs, transfer
from life, and light, to gloom, and dungeons, deep? Poor
wretches, who have, been racked, to tell the truth; and, like
Procrustes, and his iron bed, to suit the subject. It is, too
barbarous! I can, only wish, that all, were changed.

Doge.—Your Highness, dreams, again. A strong, cen-
tralized, government, for me. The people have no
rights, we would respect. All power, in our rule. The
rack, the torture, and the headsman, give us peace. Fear
keeps them down, and always should do so.

Duke.—Do you not think, the innocent, suffer, with the
guilty?

Doge.—'Twere better, to let a thousand, innocent, be pun-
ished, than one, guilty one, escape.

Duke.—Well, gentlemen, of the Council, you are dismissed; and, I thank you, for your attendance. [Scene changes.]

[Scene: In Guido's shop.]

Guido.—Now do the gods befriend; this is more than I could dream of, or could ask! My little star, so bright, now pales the noonday sun. Oh, Venice, you are free! I'll knock your fetters, off; lift your galling yoke. Hewers of wood, and drawers of water, you shall be free, to think, to act, to speak, to choose your rulers, as of yore! Guido's crusade, against oppression—Guido, and liberty, forever!

Guido.—Sons of Liberty, and the Red Cross, I greet you, one and all; and, with closed doors, we will see how stands the record, and if your work's well done; the summing up will be most grand.

First man.—The men, we have seen, are with us, soul, and body; and wait, your good commands. They are timid, and afraid to meet. The Doge's spies are everywhere. I can report for all.

Guido.—I come, direct, from this great council, and have much to tell. I have the Church of Rome's broad seal, and full protection, for you all. The Duke, himself, has given orders, that we, be not molested, and can meet, at will. Instruct the men, to talk only of this crusader's plan; when all are in, and doors are closed, see that all, are brothers, and, can give the signs. I give you, here, a list, of the Doge's secret spies. Let each one remember, they can never join. Pay them for their silence. 'Tis all we ask; you can be more bold. Work, with free hands and willing hearts. We will meet again, say, two weeks hence. [Exit all.]

[Scene: In Guido's garden. Enter Zelia, alone.]

Zelia.—Why, am I always doomed to bitter regrets! Disappointment, sits enthroned, in this poor heart, till hope, itself, is dead. My dream, has faded, like the morning mist. Oh! that Alfonso stood, before me now! The thought is rapture! When will we meet again? I have no thought, that is not all his own. Will this, soft summer air, waft but one sigh to thee, and tell that Zelia loves!

Page.—I'll be the summer air, and will not have far, to go. Follow me!

Zelia.—Lead on; I'll follow.

Alfonso.—Zelia!

Zelia.—Alfonso!

Alfonso.—Be still, my throbbing heart, be still! lest you disturb, this queenly head, reposing on my breast! Break not the trance, that binds two souls, as one—though severed far by fate; so cruel and relentless, too. Unclose those lovely orbs, and gaze upon my face. Their soft, and liquid light fills me with untold rapture! My heart is thine, fair Zelia; only thine!

Zelia.—The gentle flower, turns its sweet face, unto the lordly sun. Night, would be eternal, did not his bright, and gorgeous rays, give life, and light, to all things. I've waited long, to see thee, and ask forgiveness for my broken promise. Was all ready, for the ball, when stupor filled, my thoughts, with drowsy dreaming—sleep, quiet sleep, stole all my sense away, and, like a babe, a helpless thing, I lay, until the morning light broke, in the distant east. You will forgive me, Alfonso, for my very heart's sake.

Alfonso.—I am well repaid, my Zelia, for the disappointment, long since forgotten—I am used to such. One happy moment, in thy bright presence, would repay a world of bitter regrets. Speak no more, of this; 'tis for the present, we live—we know the past—the future, uncertain. When can you meet me, again, my fair one? Every moment here, is fraught with danger; your father's hate, would send my soul to hades, so quick, I'd scarce have time to pray.

Zelia.—I will meet thee, at any hour, or place, you name: my honor's safe, in your good keeping. As you well have said, we are in danger here. Silvia, my nurse, may come at any moment.

Alfonso—Say you will meet me, to-morrow night, in mask. (for I want not this gaping crowd, to gaze upon thy heaven . born beauty), in the shadow of the old cathedral, 'tis a lonely spot, the moon will full, and we be undisturbed. Remember, when the clock strikes ten, you can come home, before 'tis late, and not be missed. As the last stroke rings out, upon the quiet air, I'll step within the moonlight—one kiss, from those sweet lips, and I am gone. [Exit.]

Zelia.—I'll hurry to my room; poor, foolish old Silvia, will be alarmed; I have been absent, an hour, or more, already. Oh! speed the time, Alfonso, when thy loving arms, shall once more clasp me, in a long embrace. What of my poor, poor father? Is this the way a child repays, a loving father's care? I know, and feel the wrong, yet scarce can find a remedy; 'tis fate impells me, with resistless force, to happiness, or impending doom—all in the future. Who can tell, the stolen fruit, is most delicious to the taste. The interdiction of my love, but fans the spark—adds fuel to the flames, that burns, and scorches, with its fiery breath. Had I known other men, and mixed more with the world, I would be a better judge—why judge, for love is blind, and with all reason fled? If he deceives me, and wrecks my first, and only love, my pure and childish hopes, I'd wish this fatal beauty— like the Medusa—had power, with one fixed stare, upon his false, perfideous face, and with steady, gorgon gaze, would turn him, soul, and body, into stone—a fitting monument of treachery. Why doubt he loves me; I'll think no more of this. [Exit.]

Portio.—[Scene number two.]—Ha! ha! I am with thee.

still, my sweet, and noble Alfonso; one more chapter in the events of time, one more notch upon my memories stick. You are duped again; the blood hound, is not more sure of trail. I'll to my good master, and report at once.

[Scene changes to Guido's room. Enter Portio.]

Guido.—You have some news, my faithful Portio, that much concerns myself.

Portio.—You are right, good master---very right. Alfonso scaled the garden wall, and held sweet converse with your daughter; the meeting was a tender one. Zelia madly loves, this inhuman villain.

Guido.—Oh! fatal day, that brought those puppets, to my happy home, and thrice fatal the day, my daughter met them; my mind has had no peace---all is unrest. I'll be even with this wolf, in human guise. I wish not his blood, upon my hands—it is too base, and would so pollute them; I'd chop them off, and smile. I have a better plan. Let his life rust, in some deep dungeon cell, where the light, of day, ne'er casts a shadow on its gloomy walls, and with his fit companions---slimy toads, and snakes---he can repent him of the evil done: to sooth the lagging, lonesome hours, the ghosts of murdered innocence can pass in swift review, and may Tisiphone, with her scorpion lash, bring daily torture to his soul.

Portio.—You, hate him, for the evil he may do. I hate him for the evil already done. For a wager, he won, my only sister's love---poor, confiding heart---now fills a watery grave, beneath the Adriatic sea. With his own hands he slew her, because she loved him still, and like the faithful hound, did follow, day by day, his every step, that she might, be near, and lick the hand, that doled out unrequited love. These very eyes, did see him slay, a poor, old, unoffensive, Jew, because he sought, that which he had loaned. Alfonso slew him, and robbed him, of his hoarded gold.

Guido.—Why did you not report him to the council? The Sion of St. Mark would send him to the block.

Portio.—He is rich, and I am poor. Halls of justice are seldom open, to the moneyless. Broad, bright gold, would clear the basest criminal in all Venice. He is noble---I am plebeian-born. I work through you, and you, alone, can give me my revenge

Guido.—Here is my hand, and with it, hate enough to set the world on fire. The torture would be heaven to him, should he harm, my only child.

Portio.—Thanks, good master---but for my report. They have agreed, to meet, beneath the shadow of the old cathedral, upon the stroke of ten, to-morrow night.

Guido.---Enough! Portio, find Antonio, and send him straight to me. [Exit Portio.] Now, for some counter-plot ---one worthy of my brain. If I can keep my daughter from this villain, for a little while, I'll place him, where he will do no further harm. Lucretia, shall stand in Zelia's place. I'll write a note, and send by my page, at once. [Seats himself and writes.] Noble Lucretia, Alfonso bids me convey to thee, his tender love, and wishes for thy presence--- can you meet nim to-morrow night, upon the stroke of ten, beside the old cathedral? He has much to tell thee; come without fail. [Rings. Page enters.] Take this note to Lucretia; find Bravio, the gondolier, he will take thee straight to her. Deliver this note to herself alone. Now go.

Antonio.---[Knocks. Enters.] It has been many days, since these old eyes of mine, have seen thy face; it seems changed to me; deep furrows of thought, have plowed the surface, till I scarce would know thee. What do you wish?

Guido.---To save my daughter, from the fowler's snare; have thy gondola, close by my garden wall, and near the water-gate, on to-morrow night, at nine, or half-past nine; my daughter will wish thee to convey her to the cathedral of St. Mark. Go everywhere, but avoid this place, and say you lost the way. Bring her back safe, and here is a ducat for thy trouble. Now, go, and fail me not. [Exit.]

Zeno.---Here is my hand, friend Guido. I have not seen thee for an age. How fares thy conquest of the holy land?

Guido.—I have been most fortunate, Zeno, and can already count my followers by the hundreds. I want more men---am greedy, as you see; my plans work well.

Zeno.---You seem changed to me---restless as some wandering spirit.

Guido.---My preparation, my plots, and counter-plots, to keep Alfonso at bay. Zeno, I have lived a lifetime, in the last few weeks. If my plans succeed, you will be well remembered. If I fail, you will drop a tear for friendship's sake, upon my lonely grave.

[Scene on St. Marco's Square. The Doge and soldiers advance.]

Guard.—Stand aside, all! Caps off, here comes the Doge.

Guido.—What said he, citizen? Why these guards? Does he fear a tumult, in the street?

Citizen.—Take off your cap, and stand aside, to let this royal cortege pass; or the guards will cut you down.

Guido.—Do I dream? Are my eyes wide open! Can it be then; the souls of men in Venice, have become so servile, as to bow down before this Doge! Or do they fear the rack, and torture? There is no law for this!

Citizen.—You must be a stranger here, to speak, with so bold a tongue.

Guido.—My tongue is bold in the cause of right; and ever will be so! No clownish, thieving, Doge, shall ever fetter my free thought---bind up my liberty of speech! God gave us both.   There is no ducal decree that says men shall not speak! And bow down their craven hearts, to this small servant of a people, who once were free!

Citizen.—They come. this way, and if your sword's, as brave, as your bold speech, you are a man indeed.

Guard.—Why stand, you not aside?—the Doge, would pass.

Guido.—Then let the Doge, pass around; the streets, are free to all. A little brief authority, has turned, his empty head.

Doge.—Stand aside, I say, and make thee obeisance, to our worthy self; we wish to pass.

Guido.—There is no ducal decree, in proud old Venice, with its hoary-aged laws, that makes men, cringe and bow to thee, for very fear, lest they offend, thy greatness.

Doge.—So glib a tongue as thine, belongs alone to Guido, or I greatly err.

Guido.—You have well, and truly, said, and God be praised, my heart, and mind, are free as this pure air. Who are you, that men should fall down, and worship at thy feet? A little power, hath turned, thy giddy head.

Doge.—Down with him, guards. Such insolence, deserves sure death. [Guards advance—Guido draws his sword.]

Guido.—Stand fast. The man who makes, but one little step, I'll run him through and through, with this good sword of mine. The street is broad; let him pass around.

Doge.—By all the furies, why do you not advance—a single arm defies thee.

Guido.—Advance yourself, and be a man. Shield not your craven heart, behind those hearts of oak. Thy guilty soul should tremble, in the presence of this good people, you have so foully wronged. Take off thy cap, or by this good sword, we will throw you in the sea.

Citizens.—Down with the Doge! Guido, forever! Off with his cap.

[All advance upon the guard.]

Guido.—Hold, good friends, one and all; stand back; obey the law, and let no blood be spilt. Now, get thee to thy palace, and remember well, a citizen of Venice, is always free. First came wealth, and with this wealth, these titled nobles; and with these titled nobles, came this despotic Doge, and Council. Turn back, old father time, thy swift, revolving wheel, and give us good old times, when freemen ruled, and kings were slaves.

Citizens.—Guido, forever! Down with the Doge!

[Scene changes.]

[SCENE—In Guido's House. Men assemble.]

Guido.—Well, does our sky look bright, and the pathway to the gods' abode, all clear? or do the clouds, obscure their twinkling brightness? Will the storm, break upon us, and our lives, be blotted, from this ever-changing world?

First man.—The sky is clear, and all is well. Our numbers have increased, so fast, we will soon outnumber the ducal guard.

Guido.---Have you bound them, with the oath? and know they the signs? Be cautious and be bold, for kingdoms have been bought and sold. We will strike, a sudden, heavy, blow. Be on the watch, and ready for my call. To day, on St. Marco's Square, this worthy Doge, would have struck me down, forsooth, because I bowed not, my head, and stood aside, that he might pass. The people, on my side, bore down upon, his guards, and scattered them, like sheep. But for my presence, his saintly soul, would be among the things that were. They dare not arrest, me openly. I have disobeyed, no law. They would, in secret, drag me before, this dreadful ten. Some dungeon, 'neath the palace, would be, my fearful doom. Let a detachment, follow me, and guard well, the leader, of your cause. Be sure, the red cross, is well displayed, that I may know, my men—and may not, Phaeton's fate, be mine; though, like him, my aim was high, my fall, be great.

[SCENE.---In Mario's House.]

Mario.---My very soul, is crushed, with this weight of woe; my heart is crazed, and bowed with grief, to think Alfonso's false to me. Would that his dagger, had pierced my heart, and I were dead. I gave him love, and honor too, and now my guilty heart must hide, its shame. My noble brothers, suspect me not, and wonder, at my listless eye, and pale, wan cheek. I fear to tell them all; fear, lest I, lose their love---be an outcast, scorned by my sex, jeered by the men. Would that the earth, could open wide, and hide, or give oblivion, Oh, for one draught, from Lethe's Plutonian river.

Claud.—Crying again, my noble sister. What ails thee, of late? Be bright, and smile, the same old smile, that made your brother's heart so glad.

Mario—Winter's white mantle fades, the bright roses of June, that pale and die before its icy breath. Am I not, a blighted flower? I feel like one.

Claud.—In heaven's name, what ails thee? Mario, my sister, speak. You, the pride, of our fair name, the idol of all hearts, the envy of thy fair companions. These young Venetian gallants, have already crowned thee queen; or, do you wish, more finery, jewels, laces? Speak! What would you have? It shall be thine.

Mario.—I wish for none of these. Would that I ne'er had seen them; I'd be more happy now. Oh! for the cloistered life, of some poor nun. I wish only for peace of heart. It is the empyrean of earth.

Claud.—It is thy heart, then, Mario. Some disappointed hope. He showed bad taste, indeed, to prefer another, and look so coldly on thy love.

Mario.—Oh!! happy would I be, were such the case. I was the foolish moth, that fluttered too near the dazzling light; my wings are singed, to blackness. Would that I could fly, and leave thee in peace.

Claud.—What mean you, Mario? I only stumble in the dark.

Mario.—I can tell thee no more. Leave me, good brother, oh leave me. [Weeps.]

Claud.—I will not leave thee, till you tell me all.

Mario.--How can my faltering lips, repeat the story of my wrong? You would spurn me from your very presence, and from my brother's love.

Claud.--Has some base churl betrayed your love, and trifled with your heart?

Mario.—Not only with my heart, but honor too.

Claud.—Great gods! it is a crushing blow. Oh, Mario! my sister!! to think that one so fair as thee, has pulled down the honor, of our lordly house, our proud name trailed, in dust, and dirt.

Mario.—'Tis true, thou hast, my secret then.

Claud.—Who is this villain? Speak, that I may slay, and send his soul to hell—the false, perfidious wretch.

Mario.—He won my love, and then my soul.

Claud.—His name, Mario, his name!

Mario.—Alfonso!

Claud.—My best of friends. Ah, little did I think, when round some festive board, the wine, and jest, did pass, he, boasting, of his conquests, and his loves, included thee. Even now, he is on the point, of winning Guido's daughter's love, and openly doth boast of this, and wages gold, he'll win. I could laugh at him then, but now, 'tis mine to mourn. Oh, human heart, laugh not at other's woe. The same sad fate, may also be thine.

Mario.—And now, my noble brother, Claud, I'll say farewell, to all these happy scenes. I had no mother, to guide, my steps aright: to counsel, and protect. I have no claims, upon my brother's love; no claims to this kind roof, that sheltered me, in childhood's happy day; no claims to your proud name, and high position. I have lost all, and in the losing, lost myself.

Claud.—Did we not swear, upon the holy cross, when our dear mother died, to love thee, with a mother's love? to shield thee from all harm? Whatever fate betide, thee, to love, and cherish, still?

Mario.—You will not, cast me from you, then. Oh, bless your noble heart. You will not despise, so mean a creature, as my broken-hearted self, because I loved him, and with my love, disgraced your noble name.

Claud.—You are forgiven, my sister, still; we are but human—the sin that finds a brother out to-day, may be ours

to-morrow, ever ready to cast the first stone, when we ourselves, are deeply, darkly, stained with sin—the reason more
sin not, because the tempter, throws no snare, to catch the
light-winged bird. I swear to thee, my sister, vengeance on
the betrayer of your innocence. Time, space, eternity. shall
not snatch him, from my grasp. Kill as he has killed—curse
him. Oh, curse the day, that brought him to the world.

Mario.—Swear not, my brother. Kill not. Oh! promise
me, your sister, that you'll harm not, one single hair. Two
wrongs, make not one right. Add not his sinful, guilty soul,
and life, to my already heavy burden.

Claud.—I'll to our brothers, Mario, and see, what they will
say, and do. How can I tell them this? Oh, fate, nerve my
heart, and make it very steel—to save our honor. We would
sink. all Venice, and its people too. Good-by, Mario. Thy
very misfortune, makes me love thee more. Better loss of
name, and proud position, than a sister's love. be trampled
in the mire, of unchristian tongues. Keep close. Tell no
living soul of this, and all may yet be well.

[SCENE—Near the old Cathedral of St. Mark.

Alfonso.—This time, she will not disappoint, this already
exultant heart, that glories, in its very shame, and gloats
upon weak innocence. The devil, must have blessed, my
very birth. or was I the preconceived idea, that sprang full
armed, from his hellish brain? I have no feeling of remorse,
and like the spider, live for prey. 'Tis on the stroke of nine.
What makes me feel so timid? my nerves unstrung? I
thought I heard a stealthy step upon this marble pave. I
was mistaken. How could any sane mind, seek so lone a
spot? The very air is heavy, with its solemn stillness. The
shades and shadows, play hide and seek, along those pillared
walls—fitting place for the ready assassin, with his uplifted
dagger. I can almost feel the blow. He glides into the
deepening shade—one life the less, one crime the more. The
world moves on. I hear a gondola's light-splashing blade.
She comes, and to my spider's web, I've woven, with most
skillful art, ever cautious. I'll step behind this pillar—it may
not be Zelia, after all.

Lucretia.—[In cowl and hood, advances, into the moonlight. Alfonso meets her.]

Alfonso.—Most welcome Zelia, to my heart, and to this
lonely place. Though cheated in our first attempt, we will
regain the happy hours. long lost We are alone, and can
tell our love, without the fear, of this ferocious Guido—a very
tiger, always ready, to spring upon me, for my very love of
thee, fair Zelia.

Lucretia.—And you love poor Zelia, then.

Alfonso.—As no other living. moving thing. Call it not
love—the word's too tame. The very blaze consumes my

soul; the fierceness of its flame, would set the world on fire.
I madly love thee, Zelia.

Lucretia.—You have loved me, these many days. I like
not this burning love; it soonest cools, and turns to ashes on
our hands—the very passion love calls forth. You have loved
others, as well. Such love as thine, stops not at one.

Alfonso.—You do but jest, fair Zelia, and would see love's
very depth: or, are you jealous of me, then.

Lucretia.—Where is Mario? Where is Lucretia? They
tell me, you loved this Lucretia well. Do I speak the truth?

Alfonso.—She was so hard to win. No iceberg, from a Polar
sea, in all its towering, glittering grandeur, was more hard,
more freezing, or reserved. This same burning love of mine,
did melt this freezing mass.

Lucretia.—And you would cast her off, because she loved
thee well?

Alfonso.—For thee, fair Zelia, I'd cast an angel from me.

Lucretia —[Throws back her hood.] Take then, thy Zelia,
to thy heart, and be so happy in your love. Look into my
marble face, that once was fair to thee, and see Lucretia's.
Take back those cruel words, and say you love, me still; and
bid me live—for by yon moon, I swear, my blood shall stain,
this sacred marble—[Here is my dagger.]—and if you love
me not, I'll take this worthless life. Without thee, I care not
to live. Say you were but jesting, and I'll forgive. Oh, lift
this shadow from my heart!

Alfonso.—Lucretia, you well know, I did but jest, to try thy
love. Put up your dagger. God forbid thy blood, should be
upon my head.

Lucretia.—Where have you been so long? I've watched,
and waited, for your coming, till my very heart was sick.
Your note relieved my pain.

Alfonso.—My note! oh, ah yes. I have been so engrossed,
by worldly care, I had no thought of love. I am sore pressed
with debt, until my very mind, is crazed. I am a bankrupt,
and belong, to these money-making Jews. Do you wonder
at my absence? You got my note, then. Have you it with
you? I would see it.

Lucretia.—Here it is. Sweet messenger, I loth to give thee
up. [Holds it out to Alfonso. Guido steps from behind a
pillar, snatches the note, and glides away.]

Alfonso.—Hound of hell! Who was it? Gone, and with
my only clue. Oh, that I could reach him, with this good
sword. He has heard all, and could have slain me, where I
stood. I thought, I heard, a step, and was not deceived.
Foiled, again. What devil, pursues me, with such hate?
[Voice in the distance: Remember Mario, and die.] Curse
you, I'll drive you from your hiding place, and make short
work of thee. [Voice: Come on, I am still here.]

Lucretia.—You shall not go. [Clings to him. Alfonso

tries to free himself.]   I will rouse all Venice. with my cry,
for help.

Alfonso.---Unloose me. Lucretia.

Lucretia.---You shall not go. For my sake- -for your Lucretia's sake---I pray thee. listen to my voice.

Alfonso.---Unhand me, girl. [Struggles. Help! help!!
Murder. Curtain falls. End of Third Act.]

SCENE.---[In Alfonso's house.]

Alfonso.---There is some evil genius. on my track---some
messenger of the gods, whose mills grind slowly, but exceed-
ingly fine. 'Tis true I have been a guilty wretch. These
hands, that look so fair, are steeped and hardened in sin. until
my very heart is stone. All hope is gone; the world my foe;
on the side of wrong, I fight against innocence and right---
so runs the world. One half prey, on the other half. Every
spider has its fly, and weaves its ample web. I'll be the
spider---let others be the fly.

[A knock at the door. Alfonso starts back, and draws.]

Page.- -Only myself. good master.

Alfonso.---Why callest thou. me, good?

Page.---I surprised you, then?

Alfonso.---Only my thoughts. It is not good to think too
much, when one's thoughts, are preserved in alcohol, for
future reference.

Page.---Do the fires of hell, already singe your guilty soul?
Remorse, has come too late, to save thee now.

Alfonso.---[Grasps him with both hands, around the neck.]
You have betrayed me, to this stranger, who dogs my
every step.

Page.---Unloose your grasp, or I'll send this dagger to thy
heart. You do me wrong. No word of mine. has ever passed
these lips. that implicated thee.

Alfonso.---Forgive me. page, I am not myself to-night.
What clogs my vigorous mind? I tremble at a whisper. Not
a leaf that stirs, or rustles, on the tree, but startles my guilty
soul. I have been foiled a second time. Twice, as you well
know, I have appointments made, to meet this Guido's
daughter. Both times my victims stood before me. Who is
this silent foe, who works so cleverly, and so silently, deals
me out such blows? I had worked all things well: now. they
know all. and Venice is unsafe for me. Last night. I was to
meet fair Zelia, near the old Cathedral, on the stroke of ten---
and in her place, was this Lucretia. We had a stormy time.
She had a note from him, and almost in my grasp. when a tall
figure, all enveloped in a Monkish cowl, snatched the paper,
from her hands, and disappeared in those dark pillared
shades. I could not pursue him; for once in that labyrinth,
of columns, my life were not worth a ducat. I met him,
though, disguised. at the ducal ball. He told me, of my every

deed. He holds my prison key, and only waits, to close the iron door.

Page.---Have you no clue, to ferret out this foe to all your plans? It may be, this brawny-fisted Guido, to save his daughter, from thy, skillful web.

Alfonso.---It may be, Mario's brothers too, or fair Lucretia's friends. Who can tell?

Page.---I'll work up this field, and in one week report. Give me a week, and give me gold.

Alfonso.—Forgive me page. Here is my hand; stained though it be.

Page.—But a moment since, 'twas at my very throat. Well, so it is. How much, do you propose, to pay me, for this job?

Alfonso.—Fear not; I have the promise of much gold. A well-filled purse, will make thee laugh, and be my friend, once more.

Page.—Money! Oh, bright coin; golden ducats! My thirst for thee is great. Thou art the oasis in the barren waste of sand, that laves, the parched lips, of agonizing thirst. My soul pants, for thee; no, not my soul--for, such wealth, belongs to these, good old monks—my body, I would rather say; for, when this life is done, they both shall rust, in a graveyard's gloom—return, to mother earth, from whence they came.

Alfonso.---I like gold, only, for the pleasure, it brings to me. Easy come: easy go.

Page.—'Tis well, to lay in, a golden store of honey, during the shining hours, of flowery summer. When nature's dead, the body old, and wrecked, who will uphold your tottering frame—the thread of life, though almost spun? With gold, your every want, will be supplied.

Alfonso.—You live, for the future; I'll take the present. There is a still, small voice, within, that tells my soul, old age will never silver, these locks, of mine. My head will fall, before the grain is ripe, and ready, for the sickle; some gloomy dungeon, with its solitude, and clanking chains, will be my lot. Not a bright one, you would say. I'll drain the cup of pleasure, though the draining, lose me my soul.

Page.—I'll find. thy silent foe; once on his track, he'll not escape. One can learn much, from servants' wagging tongues. See that you pay me well; and money ready, when the work is done.

Alfonso.—How can I hope to escape, the vengeance, of sweet Mario's four brothers? The truth, will out. Like hounds, they will be upon my track. Lucretia, too, though peaceful, and happy, now, will soon know I am a villian. The old Jew's dying look, and money bags, are always with me. Portio's sister, a young, and guileless thing, who followed me in body, and, like the faithful dog, she licked the hand that smote her, now follows with her saintly spirit. Oh, guilty conscience; thou art the scorpion-lash, that stings my soul to madness! Oh, god-like wine, I bless thee! Give me forgetfulness, of the deeds, these hands have done. Drink deep, Alfonso; and now, for my restless sleep, and dream of hell.

[Scene: In Guido's garden.]

Zelia.—What ill-timed fortune, has brought me back, without a sight, of him, my heart now holds, so dear? The stupid old gondolier—he was the first I saw. I paid him, well, and all for naught. His blind old eyes, did lose the way. I have a broken promise to record. What will Alfonso think of me? It is fated, that we ne'er should meet, to tell our love. Kind fortune, smile, but once, upon your child! I will truly swear to make amends, to thee, Alfonso.

Guido.—My child, my darling; where have you been, this hour or more? We searched the house, the garden, and the street. It was not wise, to leave us thus. Where have you been? Speak, my child; remember, 'tis your father.

Zelia.—How you frightened me, dear father. My nerves are all unstrung. I was but riding, in an old man's gondola.

Guido.—Why, this time of night, my child? The days are long; 'twould serve thee as well.

Zelia.—I am a child, no longer. Why do you keep me a prisoner, within these hated walls?

Guido.—My, child, you are deceiving me. To think, the idol of my heart, and soul, should kill me, by untruth! You were trying to meet Alfonso,; speak, is it not so?

Zelia.—You have truly said. I love him, better than my very life.

Guido.—Better than your poor old father, whose only wish, is for your good? Think, child, of thy tender years; and with what care, the little hot-house exotic, was sheltered from the rude, wintry blast—nurtured to bloom, into goodly womanhood—and now, you turn your back, upon my teaching, to follow a fallen star, a reprobate, who would slay thee, soul and body. I've had no thought. but thee; have watched, thy sleeping innocence, with a mother's fond love. Find some one, more worthy of thy heart; not this hardened, sin-corrupting villain, Alfonso. The sigh, of murdered innocence, is sweet music, to his ear. He lures thee, to thy fall. Mario, fair Mario; come to this sweet child of mine, and save her from this awful doom! Lucretia, a martyr, to thy blinded love, come, tell this child. the ruin of thy soul! Poor, old, inoffensive Jew, come, in all thy putrid, mouldering body; tell her, how he sent his dagger, to thy heart, to seize upon thy hoarded gold, that he might win back, in game, the ducats he had lost. Poor little waif of Venice, Portio's sister; come, and tell her, of a ruined life—with what persistent love, you followed, day by day—till tired, he slew thee; and for thy love. The moan of Adriatic's sea, is all the dirge that wails for thee. Bring up thy ghastly pictures, of his deeds, till she, in horror, shall turn, with loathing, from this sin-stained monster!

Zelia.—Oh, horror! spare me! I'll hear no more of this; it seethes, and burns into my brain, until I see your ghastly pictures, one by one, in all their huge repulsiveness.

Guido.—Listen, to reason; and I'll prove to thee I speak only the solemn truth. Give me but the chance; 'tis all I ask.

Zelia.—Can he be so base of heart? Tell me, my very soul, can this be true? My Alfonso, a bloody-handed murderer? Can those soft, liquid eyes that look so straight in mine, be masks for murderous deeds? That calm, and heavenly smile, touched with an angel's white-robed innocence, does it but mask the treachery, that like a molten sea, is surging beneath? Tell me, by your hopes of heaven, is this all true? Then, why does he live? Vengeance follows him too slow.

Guido.—The truth; only the truth! Let reason sit enthroned, once more, where it was won't to rule. Drive this fatal passion from thee. Be my child again. Be Guido's child—high born, with proud resolve; and never yield one single inch, of that high-toned honor, that makes gods of men, and places them among the stars. Be prudent, distrust his motives more, and, my true word upon it, he will show his cloven foot; and for that sweet, angelic smile, a baffled demon's glare.

Zelia.—How could I ever doubt your love for me? I promise, by my sainted mother's memory, to stand steadfast as these rock-bound isles!

Guido.—I thank you my child, and on my knees could bless thee. But, oh, I fear his false, flattering tongue.

Zelia.—Stay, my father. Why come so many men, all strangers, too? The other night, I heard some strange, strange talk—not of your crusade, and the Holy Land, but treason, rank treason, to the State. Is this the object of your life? Speak; I am no child; can seal my lips to all save thee.

Guido.—How heard you, all this?

Zelia.—Woman's innate curiosity. To see them bolt and bar the doors, was more than I could stand. I know it all: will keep the secret well. And if you fail?

Guido.—The headsman's ax will fall; you will be fatherless; and, I will be no more.

Zelia.—Does this great risk, repay thee for thy trouble.

Guido.—A thousand times. To wrench all power, from this iron-handed Doge, and his subservient Council, and restore it to these good people, from whence it came, will be pay enough for me. Be silent, as the grave. My life is in your hands. I well can trust it there, and feel secure. Should you betray me, I would wish to die, and welcome death, as some sweet messenger.

Zelia.—Fear not: I am my Father's child. [Exit both.]

[Scene: In the Doge's palace.

Doge.—How like a mountain devil in my heart, is this fierce hate for Guido, base plebeian, that he is. To think, he had the power, before my people, to humble Falero, Doge of Venice, whose proud head, is worthy, of this soft hearted Duke's good crown! I cannot drag him, in chains, before the Council. He has done no wrong, broken no laws; by Ducal command, he'd soon be free. The Church of Rome secures his person from arrest. I cannot run him through with this good sword. He is the peer of Venice. How shall my vengeance reach him? I cannot kill him, with this dagger, for his band of stalwart ruffians are ever near. He goes no where. Oh, furies of hell, in all thy huge deformity, tell me, oh tell me, of some plan! Calm reason, be my friend. If I could seize him, unawares, and drag him to my dungeon, 'neath the palace, he would disappear from sight—that's all. Who could say I did it? Happy thought! I'll write a note at once. MY SON: We would see thee, on business that admits of no delay. Meet us near the old cathedral, at 10 o'clock, to-morrow night. (Signed.) FATHERS OF THE CHURCH. [Rings for a page.] Take this note to Guido, at once: leave it, and await an answer.

Alfonso.—[Knocks and enters.] 'Good morrow, Your Highness. How fares Venice, and its Doge?

Doge.—The very man, of all others, I wished, to see the most.

Alfonso.—I would be pleased to serve thee, noble Doge. Speak—what can I do? aid thee in grasping gold? You have enough

Doge.—Grasping! What mean you; an insult to my rank? Falero never forgives.

Alfonso.—I meant thee no offense. Old age has hardly cooled thy blood; be not so fiery, suits not thy silvered head.

Doge.—I was thinking of this Guido, a strange, strange, man. One would think he ruled all Venice—bids defiance to all law, and order.

Alfonso.—I hate him, though he has done me no harm, as yet. I hate him, because he is my peer, in everything, that makes men noble; but 'tis natural, and therefore human. The shafts of envy, fly, thick as hail, at those who tower above us, and make us seem so small. He will one day rule Venice, or I am no prophet.

Doge.—The burning desert sand, the sun's fierce heat, the treacherous Turk, and holy land, will be enough for him. I would he were already in the saddle, and leagues away from Venice.

Alfonso.—His followers, are thick as bees, upon a summer day. Take good care, you feel not their sting.

Doge.—How know you this, Alfonso?

Alfonso.—Use but thine eyes, and look around, and see a small red cross, upon more stout shoulders, than all the ducal force combined. Guido is master, in Venice to-day.

Doge.—This bodes little good for Venice, and I marvel that the Duke, did place such power in his hands. But then 'tis done, we will undo all this. He has a daughter fairer than the dreams of youth, and you would possess, this prize in peace; twice have you been foiled in the attempt, to meet this fair damsel. Start not, for thou knowest I speak the truth, well to my point. I would seize him unaware, once in my power; you'll hear no more of him—his very name will be forgotten, and his cause will perish too. I have but this moment sent a message for him to meet these pious Monks, who, with him, are crazed with warrior's dreams. He will, like the eager fish, take in this bait, once on my hook; 'tis joy, enough for me.

Alfonso.—If I understand thee, then, instead of these good Monks, you will have some men at arms, and stout ones, you will need, for by my faith, his muscles are only cords of steel.

Doge.—Half a dozen will be enough, and two to spare. [Knocks without.] Here comes my messenger. [Enters and hands the Doge a note.] 'Tis well, he will be prompt; when Guido's mine, you can take his daughter for yourself. My deep revenge would be incomplete without thy aid; he hates thee with no mortal hate, and taunted with possession of his daughter, the rack and torture would be elysian pleasure compared to it. Will you help me, and more gold is thine, than thou canst well loose thee in a year, by reckless play.

Alfonso.—You may count upon me, for by the gods such luck comes only once. Here is my hand, good fortune attend. I can well fathom Falereo's hate.

Doge.—I hate him, because he humbled me, before my people.

Alfonso.—How mean you, noble Doge?

Doge.—All Venice rings with the story of my shame. With a dozen, or more, of my brave guards, we walked the Square, as you well know, we came upon this Guido. All gave way, doffed their caps, but this ill-mannered churl, he gave not one inch, and stood as firm as any oak. Words followed; I ordered the guards to hew him down; the people on all sides, pressed us close, beat off my guards, and would have thrown me in the sea, but for this Guido, who, with his single arm, dispersed the crowd, and saved me from a watery grave.

Alfonso.—And for, this, you hate him, most worthy Doge.

Doge.—Not for the saving, but for the humiliation. Falereo is master in all Venice, and death to him, who dares offend.

Come take some wine, we'll drink to this fair maid, and a bumper to my hate.

Alfonso.—Wine, women, and gold, we will drink to thee.

Doge.—Throw in my hate, and with my hate, success. [Both drink.]

Alfonso.—In heaven's name, how learned you of my passion, for this lovely girl? The very danger, gives zest to keen desire, and only when the prize, is well within my grasp, will I believe I have but little luck. I count not gain beforehand. Oh! how some one has duped me, and so cleverly; twice have I made appointments to meet my unsuspecting prey, both times my old loves stood before me; you can well imagine the scene that followed. The gods, in making man, and with Promethean fire, (which was a heavenly theft) endowed him, with reason. Woman, Jove's great gift to man. What shall I say? It is enough to say, he gave her a tongue, and a will to use it, too. I retired, badly beaten.

Doge.—And you know not, who this silent worker is?

Alfonso.—I can surmise, but have no proof, he covers well his tracks. It must be Guido, to save his child.

Doge.—'Twere easy for him, to challenge thee, to mortal combat, and the tale soon told.

Alfonso.—That is the mystery. At a secret meeting, near the old cathedral, as my second love, was in the act of handing me a clue, (his letter), some one stepped from behind its pillared walls, and snatched it from my outstretched hand. Had it been Guido, he could have stabbed me, with all ease, and saved his daughter's honor, too.

Doge.—With my good aid, you can unearth this wiley fox.

Alfonso.—It may be too late. The grain is ready for Nemesis and her mill.

Doge.—Look not on life's gloomy side; cheer up, the day will surely come, and bring thee sunshine without stint.

Alfonso.—So may it be. I greatly fear, me, we will be foiled again; you know not, neither have you felt the power of Guido's fertile brain. I am reckless in pursuit of love, and gold, and yet, an unknown dread, is ever with me. The sword of Democle's suspended by a hair. The blow will fall, but when? A coward dies a thousand deaths, in dying one.

Doge.—Thy ill success hath made thee doubtful, in this good cause. Throw doubt behind thee, press on, and reach the goal of mad desire. To the victor, belong the spoils, and such spoils too. Remember, gold, and thy desire.

Alfonso.—You underrate the obstacle, most worthy Doge. You know not the man. [Page enters with Guido's note.]

Doge.—Here is his answer:

Reverent and Holy Fathers—I am ever at your service. You can count upon my presence. GUIDO.

It is enough. Once in my power, you will feel, this heavy

hand. The insult, must be avenged. Falereo, Doge of Venice, is master.

Alfonso.—I'll say farewell, and with these eager ears, will listen for some news. Send me word at once. [Exit Alfonso.]

Doge.—Well, Alfonso has gone, though not without my blessing. Oh, the thought, the inspired thought; oh, happy thought. Be still, my heart, lest you disturb this brain. Vengeance for the insult, and so soon—in such a way. I'll lacerate his heart, until the very drops of blood, shall cry out in agony. The key is mine, and woe, to Guido and his child. [Rings. Page enters.] Summon the captain of the guard to me at once. I will select this Deppo—the very man to do my bidding. He has little heart, and much less conscience, and many times has served me well. [Enter Deppo.]

Deppo.—At your command, my master.

Doge.—Pick me from the ranks, six strong, and stalwart, men. Be ready at a moment's notice. I have a secret service to perform. Look well to your arms, for by my faith, you will need them. Meet me at the old Cathedral to-morrow night, at ten o'clock.

Deppo.—It shall be as you wish.

Doge.—And mark you, Deppo, if we succeed in bringing down this game, I'll cross thy palms with gold, and a flagon of old Flemish wine, for your good men. Be on hand, and without fail. You are dismissed.

Deppo.—To hear, is to obey. [Exit.]

Doge.—As Alfonso well has said, he will be troublesome. I'll stand well to one side—I like not such danger, and am a man of peace. [Exit.]

SCENE.—[Near the old Cathedral. Enter Guido.]

Guido.—The note said ten. I am early, and well 'tis so, as it gives me vantage of my foe. I'll place my men—my ever faithful ten. [Places his men.] And now, I am ready. I could well fathom, his little plotting mind, intent on seizure of my person. He fears to arrest me openly, and would in secret, load me with chains, and send me to some dungeon— with my cause, chains, and self, to rust, and pass from memory. You know not Guido, well. I hear steps, and more than one. I'll step behind this pillar—'tis as I thought.

Doge.—He has not come yet. Deppo, place your men, well in the shade. Keep well together. When I raise both hands, spring upon him, all at once; disarm, and away with him. I hope he will not disappoint me.

Guido.—Fear not, Falereo, Doge of Venice. Guido, keeps his word—even unto death. 'Tis more than I can well say for thee. Why this decoy?

Doge.—Put up your sword friend Guido. I like not its shining blade, and point, too close. I wished to meet thee, and for the state, I have much to say. Down with your rapier point. I mean thee no harm. Since thou wilt not, then know, thou art my prisoner—and my revenge is sweet. You are mine—your daughter Alfonso's.

Guido.—Ha! ha!! ha!!! Craven—coward—come take me. [Doge raises both hands. The guards advance to seize him.] To the rescue, my men. [Ten men advance and confront, with drawn swords.] Come, take me Doge. Foiled, by heavens! [Tableaux.]

Scene.—[In Guido's garden. Enter Silvia and Zelia.]

Silvia.—Why that downcast, saddened look? You are not happy, Zelia. Tell me what ails thy heart, and mind.

Zelia.—This world's so strange, and things are not, what they seem. All is unreal. To think Alfonso so base, at heart, I cannot so believe. His smile is innocence itself; his words most fair, and father says, a villain of the deepest dye.

Silvia.—It is too true. If you desire the proof, why, proof you'll have, until your cup runs over. Try and forget him, for a more worthy heart. You cannot wreck your happiness, upon so base a churl.

Zelia.—I will demand the proof, and meet them face to face. I am no child, to swerve me from my love, because my father, and yourself, like not my choice. The proof I'll have, though it break my heart. I cannot believe him, to be so false.

Silvia.—Think, child, of thy noble sire. Did he ever tell thee falsehoods? Has he not told thee of this man?

Zelia.—He knows it not himself. 'Tis all from hearsay.

Silvia.—You are mistaken, child. With his own eyes he saw, and so believes.

Zelia.—I demand the proof, and would not then believe him false. Though other hearts be broken, he will be true to mine.

Silvia.—And when the day does come, your heart's rejected, as a worthless thing, you will then believe. Love has blinded, and your reason's clouded, by this fatal passion. You shall have proof, but if this proof convince thee not— why take the time, and trouble too, if you will not believe? We will be most glad, to furnish all you wish.

Zelia.—So let it be. I do not say, I'll cease to love. That can never! never! be, until this heart is dust.

Silvia.—If your father finds no other way, to save thee from this man, he'll throw down the gauntlet, and a mortal combat will decide for both. 'Tis easy told, for no sword in Venice, can parry, your father's thrust.

Zelia.—You mean my father will murder him, good Silvia? Then by all the gods, I'd murder him, should he harm, one single hair of Alfonso's head. My father's blood, is in my veins. He dare not do so base a thing. Let him beware.

Silvia.—You are mad—your reason's gone, to speak so of

your sire. In heaven's name, what ails the child? A father's blood upon thy hands, and cursed by man and God. Oh, horror!! such words, from those fair lips. Pray, my child; kneel down and pray, that God forgive, that murderous speech of thine.

Zelia.—I'll not believe, until the truth falls from his lips— and should those fatal words be spoken, then I'd pray to die.

Silvia.—God grant, my child, you may be spared, this pang.

Zelia.—I do not believe him false to me. Though others be cast off, my heart's as true, and steadfast, as the needle to the pole. Come, Alfonso, come. and plead thy cause. Thou art sore beset. We will speak no more of this; it is worn threadbare already.

[Enter Page.—A lady waits without, and would see thee.]

Zelia.—Gave she any name?

Page.—She gave none.

Zelia.—Show her to this place, good page.

Mario.—Pardon, fair lady, for this intrusion. My name is Mario. I came to see the face, Alfonso loves so well. You are fair indeed. I blame him not. Men's hearts are in their eyes. Once my face was fair as thine—no pallor on these sunken cheeks; no restless, weeping eyes. I have grown old, and in a month. Look upon my face, and see the fate, that will be thine. Where ever his evil eyes do fall, the thing is blighted, withered, dead. I have four noble brothers, the souls of honor, and of truth, with sorrowing hearts. They mourn a sister, though living, already dead. I was stubborn in my love for him. Advice fell heedless, on my unwilling ears. I came to warn thee, ere it be too late. Beware of Alfonso's love. I say, beware!

Zelia.—Thy pallid, suffering face, is an index of a broken, plighted faith. I cannot believe him so base as this. I could love thee myself, for thy very beauty, that still lingers, though thy color, has faded quite away. Thou art a very Niobe in thy silent grief, and would melt a heart of stone.

Mario.—I did not melt his heart, on my very knees, bowed down with woe. I told him of my wrongs, pleaded as only a broken heart can plead, that he would make amends—and for an answer, cold contempt. And were not for thy father, he would have slain me, where I stood. Why did not the blow fall, and let old mother earth open wide her arms, and receive her erring child.

Zelia.—My heart is touched with sorrow, for thy unhappy lot. You look faint; wouldst have some wine? Be seated.

Mario.—I have no time, and will be well repaid if I have saved you, from a fate so sad as mine, and if he wrecks your too trusting heart, let him not sink your soul, in deep-dyed sin; hold on to honor, though all else be lost. Kiss me upon this marble brow, and now, good-by. Will you show me out?

Zelia.—Poor, suffering woman that thou art; my heart goes out to thee. I'll heed thy lesson, it has made me strong. I thank thee noble spirit, your work's well done; fear not.

[Scene in Guido's office. Enter Mario's four brothers:]

Guido.—Come, gentlemen, be seated. How can I serve you?

First Brother.—We are Mario's brothers, and if we have no listening, tell-tale ears, we'd like to have your powerful aid. You know our sister, Mario, do you not? You know Alfonso, too; he has stained the honor, of our fair name, and faded life, and light, from Mario's heart.

Guido. I know all this, and more. If I can help thee, speak; I am with thee, soul and body, in this cause. In saving Mario, I save myself. This scoundrel, loves my daughter, too. What do you propose? I am silent, and will listen.

First Brother.—We wish to lay some plan, that we may take him without spilling blood, bind, and force him, to marry Mario, that we may save her, from dishonor.

Guido.—It can be done, and with all ease ; here's my hand upon it, we will bring the game to bay.

First Brother.—We propose to watch for this game. He frequents Signio's rooms ; we'll wait, without, and seize him, bind his mouth, convey him to our home, have a priest in waiting, and force his marriage with my sister, and with your help, 'tis done already.

Guido—I'll be on hand. What day, or rather night, shall all this be?

First Brother.—Say three nights hence; the moon will darken then; we will have a gondola in waiting, and now we'll take our leave, and thank you, as only hearts like ours can thank.

Guido.—Alfonso as a married man, my daughter, will awaken from this horrid dream. The snake, the groveling, slimy reptile, has charmed this bird of mine. I know not what to do; sweet soothing sleep, has fled these tired eyes, and well racked brain. If I can keep him, from meeting her a little while, she will be safe, and free to make a nobler choice. The cloud now gathering, o'er his wicked head, will break in torrents, of righteous retribution, and the devil call his angel home. Your time is coming, Alfonso; you will have no power, to injure innocence and truth; you'll feel Guido's heavy hand.

[End of fourth act. Scene near Signio's rooms.]

Guido.—'Tis dark as erebus, and you were right, to be most sure, I'd see thy faces. Here is one little ray of light, that comes from that cursed robber's den. Each one pass into the light, and I will do the same; 'tis well we know each other, and now to work. Alfonso is within as usual, squandering his ill-gotten gains; as 'tis on the stroke of two, he will soon pass out, and then, we'll seize him, throw this cloak over his head. Is the gondola in waiting. I secured old Antonio's, he'll be discreet of tongue.

First Brother.—I will glance within, and let you know. He is flushed with wine, and seems in greatest glee, is winning from this Signio, who keeps this place, he rakes the ducats, in his leathern purse, and now prepares to leave. Be ready and in your places. [Alfonso steps without.]

Alfonso.—The air from off the Adriatic, cools my wine-flushed face. By all the gods, dame fortune smiled to-night; my winnings were immense. Good luck attend me as well. in all my other schemes.

[All advance, and seize him, throw a cloak over his head, he struggles, is overpowered, and dragged to the boat; said just before stepping on board, cloak off.]

Guido.—Fair Alfonso, we have need of thee, in fact, thou art the central figure of the group. You should feel most honored, to find yourself in this good company; the ride will not be long. and mark thee well, should you try escape, from us, your life were not worth, one thousandth part of your base winnings.

Alfonso.—Curse you, plebeian Guido. I curse you, with the little breath still left, and curse you for all time, to come.

Guido.—Calm yourself, villain. Your curses ascend no higher, than the wicked head, from which they emanate, and fall flat to earth. You can curse no one, but yourself, and now be silent. All hands on board. [Make their exit. Scene changes to a room in Mario's house. Alfonso and crowd enter.

Guido.—All safe and well, so far. Remove the covering from his head, and now Alfonso, I'll introduce fair Mario's brothers. You see us, one and all; five daggers glitter, and thirst, for your cursed blood, a thousand lives like thine, can never atone for the wrong you've done sweet Mario.

Alfonso.—Would you murder me in cold blood, and with the assassin's dagger, too?

First Brother.—Foul murder, is too good for thee, or thou hadst been dead some time. We can scarce keep our daggers, from thy heart.

Alfonso.—What would you then, since the wrong is done, what do you propose to do?

Guido.—To make Mario some amends, we propose for thee to wed her, and this very hour.

Alfonso.—Spare me this. I have wealth, and will give it all.

Guido.—Base dog, to offer wealth for shame! You are degraded, indeed; you thought not of this, when you won her heart, and honor, with your lying tongue. You are steeped in crime and murderous deeds, until your heart is stone. The fate of Tantalus were too good for thee, and didst thou en-

ter death's domains, old Pluto, with his shadowy host, would
stop and gaze in wonder, on thy sin-poluted soul. I have
this marriage contract, to be signed by thee. It is a royal
one—no marriage bells ring out, their glad refrain; no happy
bride, in robes of lovliness, and with flowers, strewn upon
the alter of her hopes, as they take the vow, that binds them
for all time; no marriage feast, and dancing feet, to wish
them all the happiness, the world can give. A pale and
broken-hearted bride, whose wedding dress, is sombre as the
gloom of night—no faith in man—distrustful of the world.
This is the bride I bring.

First Brother.—Is Mario ready, and also the priest? 'Tis
well, let them enter. [Mario enters.]

Guido.—Fair Mario, will you pardon, your brothers and
myself, for this sad trial of your heart. • 'Tis cruel, 'tis torture, but will soon be o'er.

Mario.—My heart is numbed with grief; nothing hurts
me now. The joyless days, they come, and go, unheeded.
Would that I could sink from sight, and be forgotten by all,
or in some cloistered cell, prepare my soul for death.

Guido.—Take not thy lot so hard, suffering purifies the
soul, and time will heal the wound. Be not cast down, for
joy, follows grief, as surely as the day, the night. Come, we
but waste these precious moments, and the bridegroom, is all
impatient, to be wed. [Lays the contract on the table.] Come,
Alfonso, sign this writing.

Alfonso.—Without reading?

Guido.—Yes, dog, without reading!

Alfonso.—I will not sign it, then.

Guido.---We'll read it afterwards.

Alfonso.---Read. or no. read, I will not sign.

Guido.---Then is the good confessor here? Down on your
knees, for your time is short. [All draw their swords.] By
old charons-crowded boat, I'll give thee just five minutes, if
you sign it not then, we'll rid the earth of a monster, who
should have perished at his birth.

Alfonso.—Give me the pen; it is by force, and therefore
void.

Guido.---We will see to that. We ask not thy money,
bought by the blood of an inoffensive old Jew, nor thy base,
inhuman heart, but for thy, hand, we sue not with honeyed,
words, but with bright blades. Come, sign, your time is past.

Alfonso---[Seats himself and signs.] Well, 'tis done, what
next?

Guido.---Good father, advance, we are ready. I pray your
pardon, that we have delayed so long.

Mario.---How can I! This is terrible, and yet it should be
so. I pulled down the honor of my house, and should be
willing to rebuild. Give me strength, to stand side, by side,
with Alfonso to-night, and speak the words, that death alone

can break. Welcome shades of death, I'd be thy willing
bride. [Advances slowly.] I am ready.

[Alfonso advances. They stand before the Priest.]

Priest.—Join hands, my children; and be assured, that the
All-Seeing eye looks down from heaven, and pities thy great
woe—pours balm upon thy troubled heart, and bids thee live
anew. And by the joining of these hands, I pronounce you,
man and wife. 'Tis done; and well done, too. And now,
good night! I'll to my home, and sleep. [Leaves; all bow.]

Guido.—And, now, Alfonso, we have no happy wishes for
your future state—no banquet, of rich wine. Get thee hence;
you are odious in our sight.

Alfonso.—Hate, never-dying hate, surges and boils, within
this breast of mine, until it would pass all bounds. I swear
to live for vengeance. And, for thee—I'll dog thy footsteps,
day and night—will strike thee, where the blow falls heaviest,
and curse thee, with my latest breath! Curse you; oh, curse
you!! [Dashes out.]

First Brother.—How can we thank you enough? Without
thee, we had failed. This stubborn wretch defied thee, as it
was. We would have killed him, and our dearest wish un-
gratified. All is well! Come, sister Mario; lift up your
head; smile again, and be the light and sunshine, to our
happy home! We care not, for the world's cold sneer. The
wagging tongue of slander comes not within these walls.
Are you not glad, my sister? Come, speak.

Mario.—Good Guido! On my knees, I thank you. Not
for myself, but for my brothers, who, with the Christian
mantle of charity, covered all my sins, and cast me not into
the street, a vile and worthless thing. God bless them!
Not like the world—the woman is condemned already, while
the man is free, and stainless from all guilt.

Guido.—Arise, Mario. It is little that I have done—de-
serving no such tribute from thee—and now, I'll say good-
night—or rather, morrow, for the day breaks, already in the
east.

[Scene: In the Council room.]

Duke.—All in your places, and with despatch to expedite
the work, that comes before you! What has our worthy
Doge to say? You are at liberty to speak.

Doge.—I have much, to lay before your Highness, concern-
ing this Guido, and his band. Go where you will, in Venice,
from the Rialto to St. Marco's Square, you'll see the red
cross everywhere. They outnumber our entire force. Not
a gondolier, that plies the shining blade, but wears the cross.
The high and low, the rich and poor, alike. It has a squally
look for us, and we should trim our sails to meet this breeze.

Duke.—Suspicion and distrust pervade thy being, till little
else is left. What do you fear? They are our loyal subjects;
and, for the glory of Venice, they split a turbaned crown.

What have we to fear? Or, are you, then, jealous that it is not yourself, that leads this mail-clad host of warriors to the Holy Land?

Doge.—God forbid! My province is not blood and slaughter. I am a peaceful man; and hope, at peace, to live and die. 'Tis for thee, good Duke, I fear; and for thy reign. What should hinder this bold, and fearless soul, to place him in thy stead? He has the men and means; besides the Church his cause befriends. Look thee to thy laurels, your Highness, or you'll lose your crown!

Duke.—An idle dream of thine, my worthy Doge. I fear not for my crown. You look upon these good people, as ever ready for revolt. No truer subjects dwell in any realm.

Doge.—Your Highness has, without doubt, already heard of the rude treatment I received, on St. Marco's Square, by this knightly hero—an insult to my proud position that merits deepest damnation!

Duke.—My worthy Doge, you were in the wrong—law and justice, all with him. When you can prove to me, he is a base conspirator, against our ducal crown, and laws, I'll be the first to place his head, upon a pole, without the palace gate, that those who see, may tremble! My hand falls heavy, and with a crushing blow. Were he my brother, pleading at my very feet, I'd close these ears with wax, and sail by the syren's isle.

Doge.—I'll prove to thee, he is a conspirator, and plots against the State.

Duke.—Where is your army of paid spies, with argus-eyed vigilance; or has some Mercury chopped off his head, to adorn a peacock's tail, and yoked to Juno's car?

Doge.—They have nothing to report. I gave them express commands to watch this Guido well. Suppose we do; how will you arrest him? His men outnumber the ducal force, by odds of two for one. We would have to watch and wait our chance, like thieves, at dead of night.

Duke.—He will soon sail; and then my faithful Doge will feel at ease. Have we aught else, before this Council? No one speaks. Then I dismiss you, to meet again when we may need your further counsel.

[Scene: In Guido's office.]

Guido.—The sun has set; and, with the close of day, call all hands up. Bolt and bar the door; place a man without; let no one approach. All present? 'Tis well! What of thy work? Like good and trusted harvesters, your graineries run over with a wealth of golden grain.

First Man.—As you can see, our work's well done. The red cross floats upon the breeze; you see them everywhere. They, like the grain, were ripe and ready for the harvest—needing some bold heart, like thine, to lead. You should be cautious, and not expose yourself, too much; for, did you fall, our holy cause were lost. We'd be the most abject of slaves.

Guido.—Fear not; they do not even dream of danger; and know not the sword hangs o'er them, suspended by a hair. Their spies have been well paid by us, and close have kept their tongues. They know nothing of our plans. The time has come to strike for liberty, and right! On this day, week, as the old Cathderal clock, strikes twelve, and the shadows lengthen to the west, let each one, with his brave, and silent band, march forth, and meet me at the Doge's palace. We'll surprise the guards, and seize the outlets, without loss of life; make a prisoner of the Doge, and his most able scribe and secretary. Mark you, without loss of life, it can be done. When all have arrived, and each one in place, I will direct your movement. Bring scaling ladders. Are you all well armed? We will guard the arsenal with two detachments. How many men do you muster, all told?

First Man.—Five thousand, good and true!

Guido.—Well done. We are the masters of all Venice! While one half arrest the Doge, I, with the other half, will seize the royal palace, and make the Duke, himself, a prisoner. We outnuber thme royal force, at least two for one. The populace, who are not with us, will not oppose; and when the day does break, upon proud Venice, we will be rulers, and dictate good terms. The Duke is kind of heart, and loves not the cruel hand of oppression. Five thousand men, in Venetian eyes, will be enlarged to twenty. Remember, all in your places; and, as the solemn stillness is broken, by the brazen-throated, clanging bell, it will be the signal for attack, let each one head his detachment. Move quickly, and with noiseless feet. Place yourselves to command, each entrance to the palace. The last stroke of twelve will be the signal for attack; and now my heart is overjoyed that proud, beautiful Venice, will be free. We will let the Duke still reign. Down with the Doge—an inhuman wretch, whose ears are closed to mercy, and torture delights his cruel heart. The Council of Ten we will disband. These terrible inquisitors shall no more sit in judgment, within those halls, where injustice has reigned supreme. The members of the Council will be voted for by districts. We'll have two bodies—the upper and the lower—and give, the poorest of our subjects, fair, impartial laws. We will seize the Doge's hoarded wealth, and ease the tax. And, now, be ready; let the men march without their shoes, and with closed lips. Be prompt, and every man in place; remember well, the day and hour; for a failure, on your part, consigns us, to the shades of death. [Exit all.

Guido.—Souls of departed heroes, who fought, in Freedom's holy cause, look down, and bless our arms! Strengthen our hearts for deadly combat, and may our crusade, be crowned with laurels of success! We fight for no priceless

treasure—'tis Liberty, the common heritage of all, be he
proud or lowly born. [Exit Guido.]

Zelia.—Oh, horror!! What is this, I've heard? My
father leader—the chief conspirator of all—against the ducal
power! This night, week, at twelve, they seize upon the
arsenal. Doge, and Ducal Palace, to be ransacked; and
by a mob—my father the leader, too! 'Tis a dangerous
power to give these mobs—supremacy. No one can tell,
where it will stop. Five thousand armed men, and Venice
at their mercy! I'll see my sire, at once, and, on my knees,
will plead in tears, to stop this dangerous move. (But my
Alfonso's safe—not mentioned in this cause.) My father's
head may fall; yet, if he succeed, how proud I'd be to see
him Doge of Venice! His heart's as noble as his soul—and
both are God-like in their grandeur. I'll keep my mouth, as
close as death—for my father's life is in my hands. These
poor, weak hands! They hold the destiny of Freedom's
cradle— of life, death, and all most dear to me! Keep thy
trust well, good heart, for 'tis a sacred one. I'll to the garden—where I can breathe more free, and think more of this
plot. [Exit.]

[Scene: In Guido's garden. Enter Zelia.

Zelia.—How cool, and fresh, the air doth seem, to this
throbbing brow, of mine, that vain would burst, with
thought! Poor, foolish head; you know not what to do!
[Starts.]

Alfonso.—Start not, my Zelia; it is Alfonso. I would risk
death, a thousand times, for one happy smile of thine! Our
love is crossed by fate, relentless fate. We have never met
to tell our love. I feel you love me, as none other. I have
been reckless, wild, and bad. You can redeem the soul,
already singed with Pluto' fire.

Zelia.—Alfonso, I have heard much of thy wayward life,
and scarce could trust, this heart of mine, in thy own keeping. You would not be false to me, and leave a broken
heart, behind?

Alfonso.—I love thee too well, for that. Oh, have no fear,
my Zelia. I will be true to thee; and in proof, would marry
thee, before another sun goes down! We are in danger, here.
Meet me on that quiet square, close by the Lion of St. Mark,
this night week. The moon is full, and will look down and
bless this union of our hearts. I will be in waiting; and now
farewell! [Exit Alfonso.]

Zelia.—I'll within.

Portio.—I am still with thee, Alfonso! Why should thy
shadow leave thee for a moment? Another time you're
foiled, my angel! I'll to good Guido, and report. [Exit.]

Guido.—Who knocks? Enter! Well, Portio, you have
some news, of course. Be brief, good Portio.

Portio.—He is to meet your daughter, hard by the Lion of

St. Mark. this night. one week hence; and proposes to marry her. at once. I am off; good by! [Exit.]

Guido.—The inhuman wretch! He seeks revenge. Married. already; he would dishonor my fair name! I'll kill this slimy reptile, and be free---I am tired of this close watch--- and rid the earth of so vile a thing Who comes, again? Enter!

Guido.—Zeno, by all the gods, the very man, I would have dispatched a messenger for thee. I have much to say.

Zeno.—It seems an age, since we have seen each other. Here is my hand.

Guido.—Be seated—draw nearer. First, let me be sure, no ears but ours do listen. All is well—and to my subject. As you well know, I have this crusader's plan on foot. Five thousand men, all told. are marshaled for the foe. Is it not a goodly array? and one I can well be proud of ?

Zeno.—Granted already. Guido; but why so secret, in your organizing ?

Guido.—You come well to the point. All this array of knights. is not for the holy land.

Zeno.—In heaven's name, what are they for?

Guido.—To free all Venice, from the Doge's rule.

Zeno.—Great gods! Can this be true? It will strike them, like Jove's thunderbolt, and from a cloudless sky. They dream not, of the danger.

Guido.—So much the better. then. You have sworn to be my friend Does the oath still bind thee, as of yore?

Zeno.—It does, and till life itself shall end.

Guido.—I ask thee not (for friendship's sake) to follow my fortunes, in this fight. If I should fall, I'll not drag thee down to Hades. and its gloom. Therefore, I have not told thee of this plot. I seek not, to overthrow the Ducal throne. I aim at the Doge, and his base minions. In fact, I'd be the Doge myself, to bring about reforms, so much needed in the affairs of state. Start not. The Doge, for ten long years, has robbed his Highness, and drained poor Venice, till she stands, a shadow of her former self—a fit abode, for Neptune and the gods. Our ships, they sailed on every sea; our streets were thronged with Moors, Arabs, Greeks, and Jews. The wealth that Titan Atlas, bore upon his shoulders, was heaped within our stores. Where has all this gone? Down deep, in the Doge's palace vaults. Chest after chest, is filled, with glittering gold—grown rust with age—while Venice groans, beneath a tax that kills her commerce, and her trade. The wavelets idly wash, against her palace walls. The Rialto's dead, and Venice, too, for that. Rouse thee, Venice. Be free, and fearless, as of old. The peerless gem of Adriatic's sea, shall yet regain her sceptre, as ruler of the sea. I seek not blood to shed—not one single drop, shall flow. It will be a great surprise to all.

Zeno.—I marvel, that you did escape the prying eyes, of this Doge, and spies. You have been silent, as the lips of death. Suspicion sleeps within the ducal breast.

Guido.—But to the theme—that's nearest, to this poor old heart, of mine. My daughter, only child, what would become of her, should ill befall my cause. The thought unmans me. A woman's weakness, shrouds my nobler self. She would be adrift, and at the mercy of this cruel world, that asks, and gives, no pity.

Zeno—Mine be the charge, to keep this child, by the shades, of my kinsmen, I swear, to guide, and guard well, this treasure in my keeping. God grant success to your brave arms, and cause, and then, you'll have no need, of my true services.

Guido.—Should this head fall, beneath the keen edge, of the headsman's ax, you'll find my papers, all arranged, and with regard, to my great wealth, I'll trust it to thy keeping, and for my only child; there is enough for both. And now, a load is lifted from my heart. Come weal, or woe, I am prepared. This night week, as the last stroke of twelve rings out, upon the midnight air, five thousand noiseless feet, will climb those marble stairs; will fill those marble halls; will clamber o'er those balconies, and if all goes well, not one drop of blood, be shed.

Zeno.—Can I not help thee, noble friend? My soul, it burns, to lead with thee, this little band, of heroes, in the cause of right.

Guido.—If I am sore pressed, you then, can come. And now, good-by, Zeno, friend of my heart; good-by. When we meet again, all will be changed. Free Venice, or a traitor's doom. Farewell!

SCENE.—[Near the Lion of St. Mark. Enter Alfonso, cautiously.]

Alfonso.—Why did I select, this quiet place? The lion of St. Mark, sits crouched, and ready for a spring. I shiver with unknown dread, and feel his fangs, already at my throat. Well, may we fear thy vengeance, for like his lordly prey, torn and rent in pieces, and thirsting for more gore, he waits in grim repose, his wealth of evening prey. Fear of thee, chills my very blood, and freezes the marrow in my quaking bones. Would that Zelia were here. This cursed lion makes me thoughtful, and fills me, with evil presentiments, for the future, and something whispers softly, to my soul: this will be your last night, on earth—for good, or ill. Shake off, my soul, this lethargetic sleep; let not this cursed lion, throw his evil eyes upon me. Hark! I heard a step, lighter than the rose leaf's fall. It is [Enters.] my Zelia, by all that's good. Welcome, fair one, to this lonely spot. The sunshine of your presence, floods my despondent heart, with cheerful life; thaws the frozen ice, with which this dreaded Lion of St. Mark, has bound my spirits with.

Zelia.—Alfonso, press me nearer to thy heart, and tell to me, the love, that finds an echo, in my own. Tell me again, of the vows you made. I am ready now, to wed thee, though my father's curse be on my head.

Alfonso.—Your love is worthy, of a better fate. Come, then, as you so will it—I am ready.

Guido.—Unhand my child, base villain, or I'll pin you to the earth. I have had enough of this. Draw, and defend yourself.

Alfonso.—I am ready. [They fence. Zelia passes between.]

Zelia.—Hold, madmen, hold! Stop, this foul murder. I'll shriek, and rouse, all Venice, with my cry. Father!! spare my lover. Alfonso! spare my father.

Guido.—Stand aside—I'll make short work, of this scoundrel!—villain! murderer!

Zelia.—Hold, father. Although I love thee, with a daughter's fond love, if thou harmest, one hair of Alfonso's head, I swear to you, the Lion of St. Mark, shall tell thy secret, to the Council, and thy head will fall.

Guido.—You are jesting—'tis an idle threat, my child. Come, villain, defend yourself.

Zelia.—Stay your hands; let not blood be spilt. I have sworn, and will keep my oath. This paper tells them all. Now stop. I command you, in the name of peace, and justice, forbear.

[They fight on. Zelia staggers to the Lion, and slips the paper in his mouth. A bell clangs—both stagger back aghast.]

Guido.—And thy hand, my daughter, has done this thing. The little hand, so often nestled in mine, from childhood to this hour, is stained with thy father's blood, and for a perjured villain, who wins thee to destroy. He is married already.

Alfonso.—Your father, speaks the truth. I have no more love for thee, than for others, as fair, and would have dishonored, thy fair name ere this, did not this hellhound, Guido, thwart my every chance. I am revenged, shades of the furies. I thank thee, for this meeting; and now fair Zelia, your father's head will fall, and by your hands. Revenge, is sweet to me. I'll see his trunkless head, a foot-ball for the rabble.

Zelia.—Oh, righteous heavens, strike me with your vengeance. Thunderbolts of Jove—oh! slay me where I stand, and let me sink, beneath the Adriatic sea; and let oblivion, cover me, with all its silent blackness. Why was I born? Oh! that I could crush thee with a look, and send thee to hell, where you belong. Why did you escape, from its sulphurous flames, to curse this earth, with thy foul presence?

Had I but a dagger, I would sink it into this heart, and die.

Guido.—The blow has killed me. Welcome, death, in any shape. I am ready for the execution. Welcome, death, a thousand times welcome. Farewell, to this high ambition, that would have made Venice free, and grand. Farewell! my comrades, who stood by my side, with armor buckled on, ready, to die for me. All hope is lost.

Zelia.—Can you forgive me, my father, for this deed?

Guido.—I have nothing to forgive, my daughter. You have been deceived, and loved this villain more than myself The cruel blow is struck. Nothing, now, can save me from this fate. Before to-morrow dawns, my head will fall, and with it, Guido's hopes.

[Enter Ducal guards, and bear him off.]

Zelia.—Here I stand, rooted to this spot by horror, at the deeds these hands have done. Arise, my father's spirit, and set my blood on fire. Be ready for brave deeds—I'll rouse all Venice. He shall be saved, though Venice be in flames. Out of my pathway, reptile. Venice to the rescue!

Alfonso.—You stir not one foot, till all is done.

Zelia.—Help! oh, help!! Save me from this villain. [Portio slips up and stabs Alfonso. Falls.]

Portio.—Revenge at last! I waited long.

Alfonso.—Curse you, Portio! oh, cur—! [Dies.]

Zelia—.Portio, for the love of God, find Zeno, and tell him of this arrest; we have no time to lose, the hour is at hand. Haste thee to the cathedral, they will stop the bell. Let it ring out upon the midnight air. Fly for your life, I'll mingle with the men. Oh! happy thought, he shall be saved.

[Scene in council chamber; all seated in their places, the headsman with his ax and block; all in robes of black and masked.]

Duke—Stand forth, illustrious prisoner. What hast thou to say? Give us all the truth, will save thee from the rack. Speak. [Scribes all write.]

Guido.—Your Highness, nothing, but the truth, will pass these lips. I have little now to live for, and welcome death, as some good friend, who stops an aching heart. I am the leader, upon me let your vengeance fall. Spare my humble followers, who, with blind faith, did follow me. Our purpose was a good one; for long years, proud Venice, Adriatics queen, has groveled in the dust of poverty, under this Doge's rule: you have been misled--deceived.

Doge—Off with his head. Axman, do your duty.

Duke.—Softly, good Doge, I am ruler here; let the prisoner speak.

Guido.—In one of the Doge's vaults, beneath his palace, well secured by bolt and bar, in brass-bound chests, you'll find gold enough, to ransom all the kings of earth. If I speak not the truth, let me but meet Sapphira's fate.

Doge.----I am not well, Your Highness, and will ask your Grace's permission to withdraw.

Duke---No one leaves the room, until this thing be sifted well. Let the prisoner speak.

Guido.---I thought to displace him, and with your Grace's permission, to take the place myself. I know the people's wants; they love Your Highness, but detest and hate, this cruel, iron-handed Doge. We intended no harm to Your Highness; not a drop of blood to spill. As a conspirator, I am condemned, and calmly wait my death. See, I will undo my collar---bare my neck; be ready for the blow.

Duke---Horrors of hell!---that birthmark. What strange, unruly fate, hath drifted Guido to my shore? Whence came you prisoner? Speak.

Guido.---From the mountain side, where storms, and lightning, smote the summer sky; the very air, was filled with freedom, and this heart, untrammeled breathed the sweet name of liberty; my brother, and myself were happy then. One day a boyish quarrel---a struggle---I fell too near the brink, and all was darkness then. After months of careful nursing I was strong again. My brother fled; I've sought him long, in vain.

Duke.----Look in my face. I am thy brother. Oh! joyous day, that we should meet again---embrace me. I roamed the earth. with a murderer's guilty soul. The scorpion lash of conscience, smote me night and day, and now to meet, and thou condemned, before the law. Is there no help?

Guido.—I ask none: I am prepared to meet my death; you may kill the life, the soul of man is free. 'Tis cruel fate, to think my brother's hand, and daughter's too, have robbed me of my life.

Duke.—What say you, noble council, shall the prisoner die?

Council.—Let the law be done; we want no conspirators in Venice, to hatch foul treason, while we sleep.

Duke.—I wash my hands, of my only brother's blood, as God is my judge.

Council.—Let the prisoner prepare for instant death. [Messenger comes in.] There are some pious Monks without, who wish to prepare, the prisoner's soul for death.

Duke.----Admit them, we cannot refuse so just a boon. [Monks all file in. and circle around the prisoner. The organ plays.]

Council.---Be quick, good Monks, your time is short; save his soul---a traitor's soul. He needs your prayers. [Shouts without.]

Page.---[All rush in.] The palace is stormed by thousands, who clamber over the walls, like bees. They have forced the guards,they beat them back. All Venice is at our doors.

[Monks all throw off, their cowls and cloaks, draw their swords, and raise them on high.]

Zelia.—Saved my father! saved···. [Rushes into his arms. They Embrace. More servants rush in,] They fill the palace; Every soldier is a prisoner; we are at the mercy of this mob. They cry for Guido everywhere. They come this way; their torches flare in every room.

Council.···Oh, Jesus! save us from this mob. Guido alone can save. All kneel down to him.

Duke.···My brother, show yourself, and then they will be content. Make the Doge a prisoner. Oh! happy day for both. You shall be Doge, indeed. A royal one you'll be. [The people cry for Guido behind the scenes. He goes out. Renewed cheering, then comes back.]

Kind friends, remember well, in free Republics the people's will should be the nation's law. They should closely guard, their rights as freemen. Let not party prejudice, or sectional hate, cause thee to lose God's gift, to man. Oh! fires of liberty, burn brightly, as of yore. Peace and plenty will be thine.

[Tableaux. The end.]